"You surprise me, Hannah,"

Adam said. "I thought I knew you." His voice was as soft as the approaching nightfall. "I had you pegged as one of those women who was so focused on getting what she wanted, and getting it quickly, that she took no notice of anything or anyone around her."

He smiled in the dim waning light, and Hannah's heart *ka-chunked* in her chest.

"I'm coming to the conclusion," he said, "that I may have been mistaken."

Many moments passed in silence. Hannah didn't know what was taking place between her and Adam. They didn't touch. Didn't speak. But she felt somehow closer to him. This man she barely knew had suddenly become important to her.

What was happening to her? What was this heated magnetism she felt when she was near Adam? When she simply *thought* of him?

She had no answers. None at all.

Dear Reader,

Silhouette Romance blends classic themes and the challenges of romance in today's world into a reassuring, fulfilling novel. And this month's offerings undeniably deliver on that promise!

In *Baby, You're Mine*, part of BUNDLES OF JOY, RITA Award-winning author Lindsay Longford tells of a pregnant, penniless widow who finds sanctuary with a sought-after bachelor who'd never thought himself the marrying kind...until now. Duty and passion collide in Sally Carleen's *The Prince's Heir*, when the prince dispatched to claim his nephew falls for the heir's beautiful adoptive mother. When a single mom desperate to keep her daughter weds an ornery rancher intent on saving his spread, she discovers that *McKenna's Bartered Bride* is what she wants to be...forever. Don't miss this next delightful installment of Sandra Steffen's BACHELOR GULCH series.

Donna Clayton delivers an emotional story about the bond of sisterhood...and how a career-driven woman learns a valuable lesson about love from the man who's *Her Dream Come True*. Carla Cassidy's MUSTANG, MONTANA, Intimate Moments series crosses into Romance with a classic boss/secretary story that starts with the proposition *Wife for a Week*, but ends...well, you'll have to read it to find out! And in Pamela Ingrahm's debut Romance novel, a millionaire CEO realizes that his temporary assistant—and her adorable toddler—have him yearning to leave his *Bachelor Boss* days behind.

Enjoy this month's titles—and keep coming back to Romance, a series guaranteed to touch *every* woman's heart.

Mary-Theresa Hussey
Senior Editor

Please address questions and book requests to:
Silhouette Reader Service
U.S.: 3010 Walden Ave., P.O. Box 1325, Buffalo, NY 14269
Canadian: P.O. Box 609, Fort Erie, Ont. L2A 5X3

HER DREAM COME TRUE

Donna Clayton

Pioneerland Library System
P.O. Box 327
410 5th St. SW
Willmar, MN 56201

OFFICIALLY WITHDRAWN FROM
PIONEERLAND LIBRARY SYSTEM

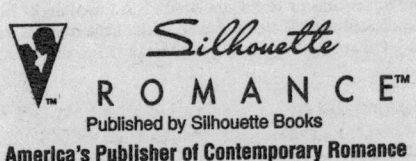

Silhouette
ROMANCE™
Published by Silhouette Books
America's Publisher of Contemporary Romance

If you purchased this book without a cover you should be aware that this book is stolen property. It was reported as "unsold and destroyed" to the publisher, and neither the author nor the publisher has received any payment for this "stripped book."

The "sister bond" is special and so very sacred it cannot be broken by time or distance or even death.
This book is lovingly dedicated to
Melissa, Susan and Reneé Jeglinski.

SILHOUETTE BOOKS

ISBN 0-373-19399-8

HER DREAM COME TRUE

Copyright © 1999 by Donna Fasano

All rights reserved. Except for use in any review, the reproduction or utilization of this work in whole or in part in any form by any electronic, mechanical or other means, now known or hereafter invented, including xerography, photocopying and recording, or in any information storage or retrieval system, is forbidden without the written permission of the editorial office, Silhouette Books, 300 East 42nd Street, New York, NY 10017 U.S.A.

All characters in this book have no existence outside the imagination of the author and have no relation whatsoever to anyone bearing the same name or names. They are not even distantly inspired by any individual known or unknown to the author, and all incidents are pure invention.

This edition published by arrangement with Harlequin Books S.A.

® and ™ are trademarks of Harlequin Books S.A., used under license. Trademarks indicated with ® are registered in the United States Patent and Trademark Office, the Canadian Trade Marks Office and in other countries.

Visit us at www.romance.net

Printed in U.S.A.

Books by Donna Clayton

Silhouette Romance

Mountain Laurel #720
Taking Love in Stride #781
Return of the Runaway Bride #999
Wife for a While #1039
Nanny and the Professor #1066
Fortune's Bride #1118
Daddy Down the Aisle #1162
*Miss Maxwell Becomes a Mom #1211
*Nanny in the Nick of Time #1217
*Beauty and the Bachelor Dad #1223
†The Stand-By Significant Other #1284
†Who's the Father of Jenny's Baby? #1302
The Boss and the Beauty #1342
His Ten-Year-Old Secret #1373
Her Dream Come True #1399

*The Single Daddy Club
†Mother & Child

DONNA CLAYTON

is proud to be a recipient of the Holt Medallion, an award honoring outstanding literary talent, for her Silhouette Romance novel *Wife for a While*. And seeing her work appear on the Waldenbooks series bestsellers list has given her a great deal of joy and satisfaction.

Reading is one of Donna's favorite ways to while away a rainy afternoon. She loves to hike, too. Another hobby added to her list of fun things to do is traveling. She fell in love with Europe during her first trip abroad recently and plans to return often. Oh, and Donna still collects cookbooks, but as her writing career grows, she finds herself using them less and less.

Donna loves to hear from her readers. Please write to her in care of Silhouette Books, 300 East 42nd Street, New York, NY 10017.

Dear Reader,

I have always longed for a sister. However, the good Lord decided I would grow up in a house full of males. With four brothers running around like half-raised heathens, is there any wonder I was a tomboy? I could climb trees and throw a football with the best of them!

Her Dream Come True is a story conjured from my deep yearning for a sibling of the female persuasion. Someone who would enjoy a little "girl talk." You know what I mean…conversations about boys and makeup and clothes. All the things girls like to whisper and wonder about. Oh, I had friends. But I can't help but believe that the bond between sisters is special. *Magical.*

When Hannah came to life on the page, I found her to be a lot like me. Pretty self-assured. Relatively competent. A go-getter. But she had her share of vulnerabilities, too. Like I said, she was a lot like me. I can't stress enough how surprised I was when I "created" Tammy and discovered she was mentally challenged. Tammy proved to have a thoroughly positive attitude, a sunny disposition, a naiveté that made her…well, almost ethereal, and most definitely a beautiful soul. Once she was in my head, I could no more have changed her than I could have forced the sun to rise in the west. Tammy was who she was…and I grew to love her—challenge and all!

I hope you love Tammy, too. And the unique bond these loving sisters share. Oh, my, and we can't forget Adam. The extraordinary man who brings Hannah and Tammy together. I do hope you flip head-over-feet for him. I know I sure did!

Enjoy,

Donna Clayton

Prologue

"What do you mean I have to go to Little Haven alone?"

Hannah Cavanaugh stared at her mother, who sat behind the massive teak desk seemingly too preoccupied with a dozen different tasks to give the topic at hand the attention it deserved. But Hannah was used to that.

"Well, I can't possibly go," Hillary Cavanaugh said, not bothering to look up from her very own handmade A List of the most prominent of New York City's social set. "You know how busy I am. If I miss an opening night or a television interview or even a silly photo shoot, that's grounds for terminating a publicity agent in a client's mind. I have to be on hand to smooth out the rough spots. You know that."

To anyone else the sigh the woman expelled would have held the perfect amount of suffering to garner the listener's sympathy; however, Hannah didn't miss the hollow, well-practiced quality in the expression.

"There simply isn't a slow season in this business."

How many times had Hannah heard that statement? How often had that excuse been used over the years to allow her mother to miss all the important events of Hannah's life?

Stop, Hannah told herself. *Mother works hard. She cares about the people she works for. She cares about you. And she's done her best for you.* Then another whispery thought nudged Hannah. *She was the parent who wanted you.*

After a long, deliberate pause, during which Hannah succeeded in stifling the sigh that threatened to erupt from her own throat, she said, "But, Mother, your husband has died. Don't you think you ought to go to pay your condolences?"

"My *ex*-husband," Hillary firmly reminded Hannah. "And neither of us has seen the man for twenty-five years. Besides, it's been nearly a month since he passed away. I'm sure the funeral is long over. Unless of course those backwoods people in that little hick town hold some sort of mourning ritual that lasts for weeks." As an aside she murmured, "Which wouldn't surprise me in the least."

The holier-than-thou tone of her mother's voice rubbed Hannah the wrong way. It made Hillary sound as if she were looking down her nose at others, judging them to be something less than they were.

"But, Mother," Hannah began, "wouldn't it be best if you were to—"

Her mother's silent, narrowed gaze burned straight through Hannah's opinion like a red-hot laser beam.

"I *am not* leaving the city. I have clients who need my attention." Hillary's sudden, cool smile didn't quite reach her eyes. "It won't take you long to get your father's affairs in order. Before you know it, you'll be back at the hospital fighting tooth and nail for that ward nurse promotion you've been working toward."

One corner of Hannah's mouth twitched. She had to hand it to her mother. Usually when the subject of Hannah's career came up, the derision in Hillary's voice was much more pronounced. But not today. Hannah suspected it was because her mother was asking her for a favor. Not that there was much actual *asking*, mind you, but with her mother, there never was.

Coming to the conclusion that the trip south was an inescapable part of her immediate future, Hannah said, "Well, I'll have to take care of things quickly. That promotion is important to me. I can't be away for more than a week. Two, tops."

"It certainly shouldn't take you that long to arrange to sell the contents of the house," Hillary said. "Contact an auction house. There have to be estate sales even in that no-man's-land down there. And then list the house with a real estate agent. You don't need to stay until a buyer is found."

Hannah grew suddenly pensive. The question on the tip of her tongue had to be asked. However, she was not eager to bring up the forbidden subject.

She'd raised the taboo issue with her mother exactly twice in her life. The first time she'd been very young, about ten, if Hannah remembered correctly, and her mother had merely brushed aside her inquiry, acting as if she'd been deaf as a doornail. The second time, Hannah and her mother had ended up having a terrible verbal row that resulted in the longest bout of silence in the history of mother-daughter relationships. Hannah wasn't wild about the thought of repeating the experience.

She steeled herself, knowing in her heart the question simply had to be asked.

"What about Tammy?"

Hillary's facial flinch was nearly imperceptible. And during the long pause, Hannah was sure her mother was garnering every ounce of control she possessed.

Without looking up, Hillary said, "You'll have to find out where she is. Check the nearest state-run institution. Find out if the state is paying her keep. I fully expect that's what you'll discover, since your father never could hold down a job for more than a month at a time."

Your father. Chills clawed their way up Hannah's spine, one vertebra at a time.

Hillary rarely used the term *your father* to describe her ex-husband to her daughter. On the highly infrequent occasions they talked about the man, they used his full name. In fact, that's exactly how her mother had delivered the news when Hannah had arrived. "Bobby Ray Cavanaugh has died," she'd said.

How had the news of her father's death made her feel? Hannah couldn't say, as she hadn't allowed herself to react. Instead she'd slid the reality of the information far to the back of her mind, put herself on autopilot, so to speak. It was unwise to show emotion in front of her mother. Hillary didn't like it. And Hannah knew her mother wasn't above using a person's thoughts and feelings against them at a later date. So Hannah had pushed her emotions aside as she concentrated on putting out the fires the unexpected news had set ablaze, focused on what had to be done. She'd deal with her feelings later.

"Once the estate is settled," Hillary continued, "you can set up some sort of spending account for the girl."

The girl. The girl. Hannah tamped down the resentment that rose in her throat as acidic as raw bile. But again she didn't react.

Her mother couldn't help her cold indifference, Hannah silently argued in Hillary's defense. Complete detachment had always been her way of dealing with the situation. However, Bobby Ray's death meant that indifference and detachment were no longer going to work.

Thoughts of Tammy seeped into Hannah's brain until they filled up every nook and cranny. And for the first time in a very long time, Hannah felt a spark of...*something* come to life in her. Excitement? Joy? She couldn't say. But what Hannah did know was that she had to get out of her mother's office before she began spouting more detailed orders where Tammy was concerned.

"I'll go to Little Haven," Hannah suddenly blurted, taking a backward step toward the door leading out of the room. "I'll take care of everything. Don't worry."

"Well..."

Not waiting for Hillary to finish, Hannah turned away.

"...if you get into trouble, call me."

Hillary's words caused Hannah's jaw to tense, her eyes to roll heavenward, and she was relieved that her unwitting reaction would go unobserved. Her mother's concern always came with the precursor *if you get into trouble*. What Hannah heard in her mother's words was, Don't bother me unless it's absolutely necessary.

However, Hannah actually felt grateful for her mother's standoffish parental technique. It was that very same aloof child-rearing method that had forced Hannah to become the independent, self-sufficient woman she was.

"And, Hannah, I don't want you—"

"I said I'll take care of everything," Hannah called over her shoulder, and knowing full well what her mother had been about to say, she let the door whisper shut between them with a firm click.

As Hannah headed down the hall toward the bank of elevators, she felt the spark of excitement flicker and grow into a full-fledged flame. Tammy. She was going to Little Haven to find out about Tammy. And if it was at all possible, Hannah planned to stop in for a nice, long visit.

Hillary would be mortified when she found out. Hannah was certain her mother had been about to order her not to see Tammy. However, she knew her recent assessment of the situation was correct—turning a blind eye was no longer the answer. Now that Tammy no longer had Bobby Ray, she would need someone.

Come hell or high water, Hannah intended to reacquaint herself with Tammy. And if possible, she was going to become the someone on whom her sister could depend.

Chapter One

Her car jostled and bumped as Hannah drove along the rutted dirt lane that led to her childhood home. Lush vegetation blocked the sunlight and cooled the dusty summer air. The jittering in the pit of her stomach wasn't strong enough to be described as a full-fledged case of butterflies; however, anxiety tweaked at her enough to let her know it could easily get to that point.

She couldn't put a name to the myriad emotions she was feeling. The memories she had of this wooded place, of the big, rambling house sitting at the end of the lane were fuzzy, like out-of-focus snapshots.

When she thought of Bobby Ray—*her father,* she silently reminded herself—shadowy images flashed before her mind's eye. A tall, gentle figure. A wide and loving smile. A laugh that was as warm and lazy as a sunny Sunday afternoon. Well...she *thought* she recalled a rich and warm laugh, but for the life of her she couldn't seem to summon the sound of it at the moment. And she couldn't recall what he looked like, either.

The love she had felt for him as a child had been overwhelming, absolutely heart-wrenching in intensity. However, she knew the memory of the love she'd felt for Bobby Ray...for her father...was twisted and knotted up in the pain and anguish she'd felt when she'd been whisked away from Little Haven, whisked away from her beloved daddy.

Stop it, Hannah! a sensible voice inside her head demanded. *Just shut the door on all that. If you don't, you'll get swallowed up in self-pity, lost in the painful past, and you don't have time for that. There are too many things that need to be taken care of.*

"Think about the house." She whispered the words aloud, as her wheels bounced over yet another rut in the dirt lane.

Shoving aside the confusing chaos of emotions conjured by memories of her father, she envisioned the house and smiled. Her childhood home was remembered as a huge dollhouse complete with a wraparound porch and fancy gingerbread trim. Over the years she hadn't allowed herself to think about it often, but when she had, her heart never failed to swell with joyful warmth. Memories of being home with Daddy in the rambling house were her refuge during the lonely times of growing up without him, the times when nothing seemed to dull the ache of missing her father. The house in her head was glowing and beautiful and just waiting to envelope her in—

Just then she drove into a clearing, and the house came into view.

Hannah gasped, her eyes widening in shock as she brought the car to a halt.

Blinking several times, she just stared. The glowing, beautiful house in her memory was in reality a shabby, dilapidated building, its paint peeling, the shrubbery overgrown to the point that the first-floor windows were obscured from view. One corner of the wraparound porch drooped noticeably. The Victorian house looked tired, just plain worn-out.

She sagged against the back of the seat. It looked as if her father hadn't lifted a finger over the years to keep the house in good repair. How could he allow his home to fall into such a state? Hannah sighed, knowing she'd probably never discover the answer to that question.

Tufts of tall grass snagged the heels of her shoes as she exited the car. She shut the door and was immediately greeted by the fattest cat she'd ever seen.

"Hello, there," she crooned as it brushed its orange fur against her calf. But when she bent to pet it, the cat raced off toward the thick trees. Hannah straightened and lifted her gaze to the house.

All at once, she became aware of just how odd the scene looked. A big Victorian house sitting in the middle of the woods. One would think a better choice would have been a log cabin or a sensible A-frame. However—

Hannah paused, her head cocking at the sound of hammering coming from nearby. She frowned, wondering where it was coming from. She hadn't seen a house for at least a mile as she drove up the main road. But then, she guessed there could be other houses hidden among the trees, just like her father's was.

There was a pause in the hammering. Then it started again. The sound was closer than she first realized. Very close.

The tall grass made walking across the yard difficult in her high heels, but she eventually made her way around to the back. By the time she got there, however, the hammering had once again stopped. She looked around, even scanned the line of thick trees at the edge of the woods.

When her gaze swung back to the house, a movement caught her attention. She looked up toward the roof.

Sunlight glinted golden off tanned skin stretched taut across a broad expanse of muscular back—bare, *male* muscular back. The man's weight rested on one knee, the other leg bent, his foot planted on the roof for balance. He dipped his hand into his carpenter's apron, where, Hannah guessed, he reached for more nails. In a flash he leaned over, positioned the nail on the roof shingle and raised the hammer in a short arc. His arm, shoulder and back muscles bunched tight, then stretched, bunched and stretched with every swing of the hammer. His movements were precise, strong and forceful, yet at the same time graceful. Almost beautiful. And his one-knee, bent-over stance was the perfect posture to show off his taut, jean-clad gluteus. The professional in Hannah refused to think of those tight muscles as anything other than what they were: the gluteus maximus. But, Lord, she'd be lying through her teeth if she said that wasn't the most perfect male butt she'd ever laid eyes on.

She inhaled a short, sharp gasp at the thought—however, her gaze didn't waver from the sight of him up there on the roof. What was the matter with her?

Again he paused, this time actually setting down the hammer and reaching into his back pocket for a handkerchief. He swiped the square of white cotton across his forehead, and Hannah gawked as the sun caught the planes and curves of tendon and sinew of his powerful upper body.

It was then that she noticed his hands, imagining the hard calluses that must surely come with such physical labor, wondering how the rough surfaces of the pads of his fingertips might feel against a woman's soft skin.

Her eyes widened at the thought, and at the same instant, the erotic idea caused saliva to pool in her mouth.

She swallowed and tried to look away. But she simply couldn't bring herself to do it.

Could his chest be as perfectly formed as his back and rear? she wondered. The question had her taking an unwitting step meant to better her view of him. But the long grass caught at her heel, tripping her up, and she let out a tiny squeal of surprise. She was able to catch her balance, and most naturally, she swung her gaze back up to the top of the house only to find the carpenter looking down at her.

Suddenly she was overwhelmingly grateful for her misstep. If he'd have caught her ogling his body, she'd have been mortified.

"Hello," he called down to her.

The corners of his mouth curled upward, his cheeks dimpled and his eyes lit with a friendly warmth. The sight of his handsome face, his charming smile, made Hannah's mind go completely blank. The reasons for her trip south slipped from her thoughts as if her mind had mysteriously become riddled with a thousand sieve holes. If she were asked something as simple as her name, she doubted at the moment if she could provide the information.

Luckily, speaking wasn't immediately necessary as the man picked up his hammer, slid it into a loop on his tool belt and then made his way over to the ladder leaning up against the side of the house. It took him several moments to descend to the ground, crucial moments Hannah used to calm the fluttering of her heart, steady her trembling hands, cool her most unseemly and inappropriate thoughts.

This was silly, she told herself. Her job as a nurse put her in the presence of naked male bodies nearly every day. Patients couldn't be examined with their clothes on. So why should the sight of this bare upper torso wreak such havoc on her central nervous system and conjure such sensual thoughts?

She hadn't time to ponder the answer before he was standing in front of her.

The man was more handsome close up than he had been way up there on the roof. The color of his eyes was an intriguing mix of blue-gray, his dark lashes making thick fanning frames. His brows were black slashes just below a strong, high forehead that was feathered with light worry lines that told Hannah he must be in his mid-to-late thirties. Perspiration from his hot work on the roof dampened the roots of his coal-black hair and glistened on the strong curve of his neck and his tanned chest. However, even though his skin had been tinged golden by the sun, the dusky disks of his nipples stood out in dark contrast.

Without conscious thought, Hannah's tongue smoothed over her suddenly dry lips, and she blinked twice, forcing her gaze to rise to his face. The humorous glint in his eyes told her in no uncertain terms that he realized her blatant appreciation. She felt her face flush hot.

"Excuse me a minute," he said, and then he moved past her. He picked up the end of the green garden hose coiled in the grass, turned on the spigot, bent over and doused his upper body with water. He ran his free hand over his chest, shoulders and the back of his neck. He rubbed at his face and combed his fingers through his hair, washing away the sweat from his body.

The blue jeans and work boots he wore kept his state of undress from being described as anything near indecent, still Hannah felt like some kind of sexual voyeur watching a very intimate act. A vivid image flashed through her mind, and she imagined her dream self taking the garden hose from his hand, directing the water to sluice over his chest as she smoothed her fingers over the massive shoulders.

The daydream came and went in a fraction of a second; however, she found it so utterly shocking that she squeezed shut her eyes and murmured, "You are going out of your mind."

"Pardon?"

He'd turned off the water and tossed the end of the hose aside. Hannah watched him dry off his face and chest with his handkerchief, and then he reached down and picked up a T-shirt that lay in a heap on the lawn.

Say something, Hannah, she silently ordered. Talk about the weather, anything, just say *something* that won't make this man think you're totally insane.

"I said the day is just fine."

Sunlight sparkled like jewels off the fat water droplets that clung to his hair. One particular liquid pearl ran along the outside edge of his ear, hovered for a moment on the bottommost curve of his sexy lobe, and then the sheer force of gravity caused it to splash onto his sun-bronzed shoulder. The instant the droplet hit, Hannah actually started, her blinking gaze lifting to his face.

Amusement twinkled in his eyes, and Hannah was left to wonder just how long she'd studied that glistening pellet. Her embarrassment grew, prickling every inch of her skin with a heated self-consciousness. And she could tell from his expression that he was enjoying her discomfort—*very much*.

What in heaven's name was wrong with her? She was normally a serious, no-nonsense kind of person. A woman who would never gawk at a man. Not under *any* circumstances.

However, it wasn't entirely her fault, she decided. If he'd get himself dressed, cover up that broad expanse of bare skin he was exposing, then she could keep her mind on more important issues like...his identity and what the heck he was doing here working on her father's house, and who had given him permission to—

The thoughts bombarded her, pushing her to speak. "Who are you? And what are you doing here?"

Adam wasn't able to completely suppress the chuckle that rumbled in his chest and tugged at his mouth. Evidently, the woman was taking on a defensive stance to cover up the blatant flirty looks she'd been giving him. In an effort to hide his humorous reaction to this new behavior of hers, he stuffed his arms into the sleeves of his cotton shirt and then took his time pulling it over his head.

He'd gotten quite a kick out of how the beautiful strawberry-blonde had been seemingly unable to take her gorgeous green eyes off his body. The current he felt sparking from her had been something akin to summer heat lightning, and it had been a long while since he had experienced its like.

After tugging the hem of the shirt, he combed his fingers through his wet hair.

"I'm Adam," he told her. "Adam Roth. And I was up there fixing the roof."

She planted her small fist on her narrow waist. "Well, I figured out you were fixing the roof. But why?"

This time his grin simply refused to be subdued as he obligingly supplied the obvious. "Because it leaked."

Her wide, very kissable mouth puckered in total frustration, and Adam felt the urge to laugh, but he didn't think it wise.

She was doing a commendable job, he decided, of keeping her gaze directed on his face; however, he knew without a shadow of a doubt that what she really wanted was to let her eyes roll up and down the length of him. It wasn't entirely conceit that made him think this, it was the simple fact that, as they stood talking, her gaze would dip to his nose, then raise to his eyes, then it would dart to his mouth and raise again to his eyes. Her gaze had so far gotten as low as his chin.

The truth of the matter was, he found her obvious attraction to him pretty ego boosting, to say the least.

His silly answer to her even sillier question had made anger spark in her clear green eyes, and Adam decided the heated emotion only made her all the more beautiful.

"Pardon me," she said, keeping her voice under tight control. "It seems as if I didn't make myself clear. What I meant was, under whose direction were you up there fixing the roof?"

What was this? he wondered. An inquisition?

The suspicion in her tone took the edge off his humor. Hell, it did more than that. It pretty much grated on his nerves.

"Before I answer that," he said, shifting his weight onto one foot and crossing his arms over his chest, "I think I'd like to know who's asking."

Chapter Two

The man was infuriating! Who did this carpenter, *this handyman*, think he was, to be questioning her right to inquire about his identity and what he was doing to her father's house? The man was simply infuriating!

"Look," she said, "I don't know who you are, but—"

"I already told you who I am," he quietly informed her. "I'm trying to find out who *you* are."

For some odd reason Hannah felt a sudden reluctance to give this man any information about herself. However, she doubted he would be satisfied until she told him *something* about her presence here in Little Haven.

"I've come from New York." Her tone was stiff. "To arrange the sale of the house and its contents. Now, if you don't mind, would you please tell me who authorized your work and how much you expect to be paid."

His eyes narrowed ominously as she spoke, and Hannah was only barely able to squelch the urge to back up a step.

"What did you say?"

She searched his face, wondering exactly which piece of the information she'd just disclosed had so thoroughly changed his demeanor. She was sure it must have been the fact that she'd cast a heavy shadow on the issue of his payment for the roof job.

"I think it's only fair for me to know just how much this is going to cost me," she said, "*before* I agree to pay, don't you?"

Obvious irritation tensed his jaw muscle. His voice lowered to a grumble as he said, "I was never expecting to be paid."

Hannah's mouth pursed almost of its own volition, but before she could express her skepticism, he continued.

"You can't sell the house," he said.

Ah, she thought, *so that was what had upset him.*

"What about Tammy? What's going to—"

His mention of her sister sparked the flame of Hannah's excitement—an excitement she couldn't quell. "You know my sister? You know where she is?"

"Your *sister?*"

"You know where I can find Tammy?"

"You're *Hannah? Hannah Cavanaugh?*"

"Can you tell me where she's living?"

"You're Bobby Ray's oldest girl?"

Neither one of them was really listening to the

other, so focused were they on working out the confused facts of the situation.

"Wait!" Hannah finally cried, lifting her hand, palm out, toward him. "Stop."

It quickly became clear to her that she wasn't going to get any useful information out of this man if she wasn't willing to make him understand who she was and why she was here.

She heaved a sigh, her overwhelming curiosity about Tammy would have to wait. At least for a few moments.

"Yes," she told him. "I'm Hannah Cavanaugh. Bobby Ray was my father. I've come from New York to pack up his personal belongings. I'm going to sell the furniture and the house and put the money away to ensure Tammy's living arrangements."

"You can't do that—" The thought was cut off as another, evidently more significant, began rolling off his tongue. "What do you mean you're going to 'ensure Tammy's living arrangements'? Why does she have to move at all?"

"Oh, I hadn't planned to move her," Hannah assured him. "She can stay right were she is. I don't want to do anything that will upset her."

"Well, you're going to upset her—" his voice tightened with anger as he added "—and you're sure as hell going to have to move her if you sell the house."

Hannah felt blindsided by the surprising revelation. "She's living *here*?"

The handy man gave a curt nod.

"B-but," she stammered, "I was under the assumption that she...I was told to look for her..." She gazed off at the tree line, trying to regain her composure. After a moment she looked back at Adam Roth. "Tammy lived with my father?"

"For all the years I've known them."

She shouldn't feel jealous. She *shouldn't*. She'd had a perfectly fine childhood. She'd been raised by a responsible parent. One who had wanted her. She was physically and mentally healthy, and for that alone Hannah knew she was far more blessed than her sister.

However, discovering that her father hadn't put Tammy in an institution, as Hannah had been told, finding out that he'd allowed his youngest daughter to live at home when he hadn't allowed his oldest to do the same was more than just disturbing for Hannah. It was earth-shattering.

Why? How could a father choose one daughter over another?

Unshed tears scalded the backs of her eyelids. She would not cry. Not in front of this stranger. Inhaling a deep, soul-steeling breath, Hannah shoved aside the cyclone of chaotic emotions that swirled around her.

"Who's been staying with Tammy since Bobby Ray died?" Her voice sounded tiny and unsure, even to her own ears, and she hated the weakness she heard in it.

"No one."

His answer shocked the life back into her. "How can that be? My sister is...special. She's—" Hannah paused and then forced herself to be more explicit. "She's retarded."

Disapproval turned his eyes slate-gray. "I think the

politically correct term in these enlightened times is *mentally challenged.*"

Hannah's face flamed hot. "Well, whatever the term, Tammy shouldn't be staying here on her own. She can't possibly be capable of taking care of herself."

"Tammy's got plenty of friends," he said. "People around here watch out for her." He cocked his head to one side. "I think you should give yourself some time to get to know your sister before you start making decisions that will impact the rest of her life."

Hannah's spine straightened. When she wanted advice from Mr. Adam Roth, she'd ask for it.

"Time," she said, stiffly, "isn't something I have a whole lot of. I have to get back to New York as soon as possible. I'm up for promotion. I'm a nurse, and I could very well become the youngest ward nurse in the hospital." An odd awkwardness crept over her for having revealed so much about herself—about her hopes and dreams—to this stranger. But he needed to know. Tipping up her chin, she boldly continued. "This might not sound like a big deal to you. But it is to me. A very big deal. I'm only telling you this to make you understand why time is of the essence. I have a lot to do and very little ti—"

"Well, you sure had plenty of time just a moment ago to eye me up like I was a prime hunk of rump roast and you were chef of the day."

She gasped, her eyes widening. "I did no such thing—"

"Ms. Cavanaugh, if you don't mind my asking," he cut in again, "where's Tammy's mother? Shouldn't *she* be the one making the decisions about the estate? She's the person to whom we wrote the letters.''

A deep frown bit into her brow. She'd been momentarily mortified by his flippant "rump roast" remark, but what he was insinuating melted away all the embarrassment and confused her to no end. "Letters? As in, more than one?"

"Three to be exact," he told her. "One every eight to ten days since Bobby Ray died. Hank Tillis and I thought—"

"Tillis." Hannah whispered the name, mulling over the familiar sound of it in her mind. "You mean the lawyer, Henry Tillis?"

"That's the one. He goes by Hank to his friends."

"My mother showed me a letter from him dated this past Monday."

"That must have been letter number three." Again, disapproval turned his gaze stormy.

Her mother had received three letters before she'd acted? Hannah couldn't believe it. But then again, maybe she could.

"You see," she began, "my mother is a very busy woman. She's a publicity agent. In New York City. Her clients need her. They depend on her. And they keep her busy. Her work makes it very hard for her to leave town...."

In that instant, Hannah was whisked back into her childhood where she relived a hundred awkward moments when she was forced to explain her mother's absence to teachers, choir directors, Brownie troop leaders, even to the parents of her friends who never seemed to miss a performance night or a fashion show or the innumerable other events a child is involved in.

You are thirty years old, Hannah, she firmly told herself. *Stop feeling obliged to make excuses. Heaven knows you don't owe Adam Roth any.*

"Look," she said, keeping her tone measured yet firm, "I'm here to see to things. Tammy has me now. And I have a well-thought-out plan. Thank you for your concern, but my sister won't be needing it any longer." Her amiable smile bordered on superficial and she knew it. "That is, of course, *if* you've finished the repairs on the roof."

He tossed her a withering look. "The leak is fixed."

"Good." She brightened even further, dismissing him by saying, "Now, you feel free to send me a bill for your work. But you'll need to get it right to me, I don't expect to be in Little Haven for long."

His face was hawkishly handsome, she decided, even under the strain of discontent.

"Don't think you can get rid of me that easy," he told her. "The people in this town aren't going to let you come to Little Haven and tip Tammy's world off its axis. If you aren't careful, you'll send that child into a tailspin."

He turned on the heel of his leather work boot and stomped off across the grass.

Hannah could have called after him. She could have informed him that she didn't need his warnings. That he had no rights here whatsoever. And neither did anyone else in Little Haven for that matter. But she didn't say any of these things. She was just glad to see the last of Adam Roth.

In fact, she was so relieved to see the man go that she wasn't the least bit aware of how her gaze had latched on to his arrogant, sexy swagger until she'd lost sight of him when he'd turned the corner of the house. Had she been aware of the hungry manner in which she'd stared, she'd have had to admit to wearing one of those imaginary tall, white hats designating her culinary chef of the day.

Adam unbuckled his tool belt, tossed it onto the worn seat and then slid behind the steering wheel of his ancient, battered pickup. He was fuming inside. Fuming to the point that he wouldn't have been surprised to see smoke coming out his ears if he were to glance at his reflection in the hazy rearview mirror. He felt like a caged grizzly bear who had been poked and prodded with a pointy stick.

Bobby Ray's family had finally responded to the letters that had been sent. And Hannah Cavanaugh had come to town.

Despite his anger, a vivid image flashed before his eyes. He'd been up on the roof when a noise down below in the yard had caught his attention. At first glance, he'd thought the woman had been Tammy. But he soon discovered he was wrong.

For the rest of his life the image of Hannah Cavanaugh standing on the back lawn would be burned into his brain; the golden, midday sunlight gleaming on her coppery-blond hair, the royal blue of her form-fitting dress complimenting her milky skin to perfection, her high-heeled shoes showing off shapely calves. She'd been a dazzling spectacle he wouldn't soon forget.

However, the fact that she was a stunner didn't make her any less irritating.

He couldn't believe she actually meant to waltz into Little Haven and upset Tammy's whole existence. Granted, Tammy was no child. At least, not in the state's eyes. She was twenty-four, and had the height and build of a woman to prove her age. However, in her mind she was young and innocent, extremely naive and in need of protection.

Hannah Cavanaugh had referred to her sister as "special" and that was an apt description for Tammy. Adam would be damned if he allowed Bobby Ray's oldest daughter, or his ex-wife, to hurt the extraordinary young woman. He'd made a promise to Bobby Ray, and he meant to keep it.

Adam realized he was going to have a battle on his hands. He had no legal rights. Hank had warned him of that, over and over. But Adam didn't care. He'd given his word to Bobby Ray. And to Adam, a man was only as good as his word and his reputation.

As he made his way down the rutted lane that would take him to the main road, a vivid picture of Hannah Cavanaugh flashed before his eyes. He may never have met the woman before today, but he knew her. Or rather, he knew her like. High-handed feminists. They came rushing into every situation so intent on fixing things, they never stopped long enough to see if those things were even broke. And the mending and adjusting they did always benefited themselves more so than anyone else.

He'd met more than his share of tyrannical, self-centered women in college and again during his political career in Philadelphia. Hell, he'd even married one of them and tried to make her happy. But he'd quickly discovered that doing so was an impossible feat. A sound of disgust rushed from his lips. Some women were so caught up in success and careers, so focused on what they intended to squeeze out of the world at large, that they couldn't see or understand what was going on around them.

Hannah Cavanaugh had said she had to get back to New York where, she'd intimated, she had an all-consuming career to get back to. He doubted she had a husband. Or children. Nope. He highly suspected she was far too focused on herself for that.

Well, he had news for the beautiful Hannah. He was making a vow, here and now. One way or another he was going to toss a wrench into those nicely greased cogs she called her plan.

A plan? A plan? Had she really told Adam Roth that she had a well-thought-out plan?

Well, she might have arrived in Little Haven with a strategy: sell the house and furniture and procure long-term housing arrangements for Tammy. However, discovering that her sister wasn't living in an institution had changed everything.

Hannah paced across the kitchen's worn linoleum floor as she waited for Tammy. She'd found a note taped to the rickety screen door. Apparently her sister had written it to let visitors know she'd "Gon fishing." And that she'd "Be bak soon." And then Tammy had signed her full name.

A smile had pulled at Hannah's mouth when she'd read her sister's carefully printed, block-lettered words. Hannah was pleased to learn that Tammy could write. And if she could write, she could surely read. At least at an elementary level, anyway.

It was the note that had made Hannah realize how little she knew of her sister. All she had were a few perceptions that had been based on little, and sometimes no, information. The one time she'd forced her mother to talk about Tammy, Hannah had been disturbed by what she'd learned...and what she'd learned hadn't been much, before the incident had turned into a huge argument.

So Tammy was a stranger. And Hannah only had a week, two at the most, in which to garner her sister's trust.

The thought was daunting.

If you aren't careful, you'll send that child into a tailspin. Adam Roth's words floated through her mind like an immutable echo.

What did *he* know? Nothing, that's what. Hannah was here to help Tammy. And she wouldn't let Adam Roth, or anybody else for that matter, keep her from her goal.

Afternoon sunlight filtered through the grimy window. Dust floated in the hot, dry air. The curtains were faded and dingy and full of what looked to be weeks' worth of dust.

This place needed a good cleaning, and since she could just as well ponder another plan while she was washing a few dishes and wiping down the countertops as she could standing idle, Hannah set to work.

After washing what she guessed were Tammy's breakfast dishes, she scrubbed the tabletop and the counters, too. Then she spent a full thirty minutes wiping down the massive stove. The thing was an ancient monstrosity. Hannah guessed it was one of the very first models of gas ranges ever to be manufactured.

While she rubbed at the accumulated grease, she mulled over how she would deal with this new situation. She didn't want to upset Tammy by selling the house. But Hannah didn't see any way around it. She couldn't very well leave her sister here in Little Haven all alone.

Learning that Tammy had been on her own here in this house since Bobby Ray's death made Hannah feel horribly guilty. Had her mother really received three letters alerting her to her ex-husband's death before she'd responded? Hannah shook her head. Well, she did know her mother had thought Tammy was safe and sound in a state home.

Hannah shook the curtains out on the back porch, scrubbed the grime from the window and then hung the curtains back on their rods. And as she attacked the floor with a broom and then a mop, she continued to reflect on what she should do about her father's estate and Tammy's living arrangements. Maybe her mother could give her some advice.

No, came a firm, silent reply. You can handle this. Besides, every single time you ask for her guidance you always end up regretting it.

Before Hannah realized it, the sunlight was casting long shadows across the floor. The linoleum was too worn to shine, but at least she knew it was clean.

Where could Tammy be? she wondered, glancing out the now-crystal-clear window.

Hannah's skin felt hot and tacky with dust and dirt. She went to the front of the house and up the long staircase to find the bathroom. Somehow, she just knew the house didn't have one on the first floor.

When she stepped up onto the second-floor landing, it was like a fist struck her square in the solar plexus. She looked at the three open bedroom doors, hazy childhood memories flooding her brain.

A little girl's laughter echoed in the silent, stuffy air. Squeals of utter delight danced a jig around her. Wraithlike giggles raced from the master bedroom to the one Hannah remembered as being her own, chased by a deeper, more masculine laugh.

The experience wasn't frightening in the least. Because Hannah knew without a doubt that what she was hearing was in her mind. Sounds conjured solely by her imagination. Memories of happy times with her father when she was a toddler.

The delighted sounds she heard were the remnants of joyful moments she'd spent with the one person she'd loved more dearly than all others.

Before she even realized what she was doing, Hannah had pushed open the door of the master bedroom. She took a step inside and then another.

The same wrought-iron bed sat at one side of the cramped room, the heavy walnut dresser at the other. Hannah grinned, remembering how her father had chuckled at her while she'd jumped on that bed, making the coils squeak and groan. But he would always shoo her off the mattress when the sound of her mother's footsteps were heard on the stairs. He'd chase her then, from his room to hers, where he'd tuck her into bed and sing her a lullaby.

"Oh, Daddy." The words were wrenched from her throat, like rusty nails being torn from a piece of dry-rotted wood. Hot tears of sorrow seared her eye sockets and blurred her vision.

Why had he sent her away? Why had he made her go with her mother, when all she'd wanted to do was stay here with him?

Reaching up to smooth back a strand of her hair, movement caught her eye and she swung her gaze to the left and saw her reflection in the mirror.

What is the matter with you? she chided.

She wasn't a little girl anymore. And she'd never find answers to her questions. The possibility of that had died and was buried with her father.

Using the fingers of both hands, she rubbed away her tears. She needed to set the grief away from her. Far away from her. Surely Tammy would be home soon. How would the poor girl react to finding a sobbing, disheveled woman in her house?

"Get yourself washed up," she ordered her reflection, feeling more in control with the renewed strength she heard in her tone. "You want to be ready when your sister arrives."

Water from the bathroom sink was cool as she splashed it over her face and arms. She'd found a washcloth on a shelf and used it to scrub away the dust and perspiration on her skin. She was rinsing out the cloth, intending to hang it up to dry, when she heard the screen door open and then shut with a bang.

Hannah moved into the hallway and then to the stairs. She paused, her hand resting on the top of the newel post. Her heart pounded in her chest. Even though she had no idea what to expect, regarding just how mentally alert her sister would be, Hannah was so excited at the thought of seeing Tammy again.

However, at the same time she felt a tinge of fear creep over her.

What if Tammy didn't like her?

Stop it, she told herself. She'll like you. She's your sister.

She'll like you, the voice silently continued, *if you don't scare the poor child half to death.*

Hannah's eyes went wide with the sudden thought. Tammy would surely be frightened to death finding someone—a complete stranger—in the house.

Keeping her steps as light as possible, Hannah crept down the stairs. She heard her sister moving about in the kitchen. And then Tammy began to sing. The angelic sound filled Hannah with warmth, and she stopped in the middle of the living room to listen. She recognized the tune as an age-old religious hymn.

"Amazing grace, how sweet the sound..."

A loving smile tugged at the corners of Hannah's mouth. Indecision fought a quick battle inside her—she wanted to interrupt, yet at the same time she wanted to remain where she was and listen to the beautiful song. After only a fraction of a moment, Hannah's eagerness to meet her sister prevailed.

"Tammy?" she said softly, taking a tentative step across the threshold of the kitchen doorway.

The young woman spun around from where she stood at the sink, her gem-green eyes never losing a single measure of their merry twinkle at the sight of this stranger.

"Hi," Tammy said, her tone expressing not fear at all but a marvelous and pleasant surprise.

Hannah's breath caught in her throat. Her sister was lovely. No, she was absolutely beautiful. There was something...unearthly, almost ethereal, about the young woman.

Waves and waves of liquid gold trailed over Tammy's shoulders and down her back. She hadn't inherited the coppery-colored hair that Hannah had, hers shone a bright flaxen and was thick as could be. As Hannah looked closer, she guessed the ethereal quality she'd first noticed had to do with the innocence she saw in her sister's gaze. A purity of heart, a guilelessness that was clearly evident at first glance.

"Hello," Hannah said, her voice trembling with deep emotion. Memories of holding Tammy as a baby came to her...the only memories she had of her sister.

"I went fishing."

Hannah nodded. "I know. I read your note."

"Oh," Tammy said. "I caught lots of trout. Enough for dinner." Her face took on a dreamy expression. "Trout is my one weakness."

Her face brightened as though an idea flashed in her head like a lightbulb.

"I even caught enough so that Mrs. Blake could have some for her dinner." She grinned. "She thanked me for bringing them to her. It's a long walk to her house."

Tammy was so pleased with the notion of her good deed that Hannah had to chuckle.

"It was awfully nice of you to share," she said.

Suddenly Tammy's forehead crinkled with a frown. "Mrs. Blake is blind."

Feeling the need to commiserate, Hannah commented, "Aw, that's a real shame."

The young woman stuck her index finger up in warning. "But don't go helping her *too* much. 'Cause she'll snap your head off." Then she nodded, knowingly. "Mrs. Blake is very independent. It's best to wait until she asks you to do something for her."

At a loss for how she should respond, Hannah simply said, "I see...I'll keep that in mind."

Suddenly Hannah realized that Tammy hadn't seemed the least bit interested in her identity. Like finding a stranger in the house was no big deal. That worried Hannah. Terribly. Apparently her sister lacked the all important protective instinct that was meant to keep her safe.

"Tammy," she said softly, "do you know who I am?"

A quirky smile was the young woman's first reaction.

"Silly," Tammy said. "How can I know you when we just met?" Without waiting for a reply, she commented, "I'm hungry. Are you hungry?"

"But aren't you concerned," Hannah went on, "coming home to find a stranger in your house?"

Tammy shrugged. "You cleaned up really good. The kitchen looks wonderful." Wrinkling her nose, she admitted, "I hate to clean." Her smile returned. "I figured I should be nice."

Hannah found this the most puerile thinking. Quietly she asked, "How do you know I was the one who cleaned the kitchen?"

Her sister's innocent green eyes blinked. After a long moment she asked, "You did, didn't you?"

Frustration welled up in Hannah. "Well...yes, but that's not the point. You should be careful. How did you know I wasn't going to hurt you? Or steal from you? Or something?"

"Oh, I knew," Tammy assured her. Then she glanced over her shoulder where the fish fillets lay on the counter by the sink. "Are you hungry? I'm really hungry."

"Okay, okay," Hannah said. "You sit down and I'll cook the fish."

She shooed Tammy away from the counter and looked down at the snowy-white fillets. Working in the hospital fifty to sixty hours a week didn't leave much time for cooking, but how hard could it be to—

"I like baked beans with my fried trout," Tammy said from her seat at the table.

"You mean like pork and beans? From a can?"

Tammy nodded, pointing to the cabinet next to the stove. Hannah pulled the door open, and sure enough, she found rows of canned vegetables. She extracted one can of beans.

"And you like your fish fried?"

"Yes," she said. Then she wistfully added, "Trout is my one weakness."

Hannah couldn't stop the smile that stole across her lips. "I know," she said softly. "You told me."

After she found flour and salt and pepper for the fish, and a can opener for the beans, Hannah set to work. She wondered how she could explain to Tammy who she was and why she'd come. Easing into the issue seemed like the best solution.

"You know, Tammy," she began, "I've come from New York City to see you."

"I've never been to New York City before. Where is that, anyway? Is it far from here?"

"Oh, it's pretty far," she said. "It's a few hours' drive from here."

"Oh."

While the iron skillet heated up, she dusted the trout with flour and seasoned it with salt and pepper. Once the butter began to sizzle, Hannah placed the fish in the pan.

"I'm Hannah," she finally disclosed. "Your big sister. Did you know you have a sister?"

Holding her flour-coated fingers well away from her dress, she looked at Tammy to see the young woman's reaction to the news. However, it was like her sister hadn't even heard a word she'd said. She was too focused on the food Hannah was preparing.

"Are you gonna doctor up the beans?" Tammy shyly asked.

Hannah watched as a worried frown planted itself in her sister's brow.

"Doctor them up?" Hannah didn't quite understand.

"With some brown sugar and a tiny dollop of yellow mustard," Tammy suggested. "And a little molasses wouldn't hurt."

"I can do that," Hannah said, wiping her fingers on a tea towel. She opened cabinet doors, searching for ingredients.

Apparently Tammy felt a little more relaxed about the food preparation, because she boldly commented, "You can't be Hannah. My sister's just a little girl. She's six."

"Well..." Hannah grew silent, paused for a second. "I'm an adult now. I'm thirty years old."

Tammy's expression clearly conveyed that she

thought *that* piece of information was proof to back up her own argument, not Hannah's.

"I have Hannah. I can show you."

"What do you mean you *have* Han—"

Before she was able to complete her question, Tammy had raced off into the living room and her footsteps could be heard on the stairs.

How was she going to explain? Hannah wondered. How do you illustrate the concept of growing up to someone who had the mentality of a young child?

Going to the refrigerator, Hannah bent over and perused the contents, looking for a jar of mustard.

"Oh, oh, oh."

The panic in Tammy's voice as she rushed back into the kitchen had Hannah twisting around from the refrigerator. The thick black smoke billowing from the skillet on the burner made her eyes widen in alarm.

"Oh, my!" Hannah snatched up a pot holder that was hanging on a hook near the stove, grabbed the searing-hot pan and dropped it into the sink. She turned on the faucet. Water hissed and bubbled loudly when it hit the hot metal, and a surge of sooty steam only added more haze to the air. The smell of burned fish made Hannah raise her hand to cover her nose, and the acrid smoke made her eyes water.

"Well, *somebody* has certainly ruined dinner."

Hannah looked through the smoke to see that the irritating Adam Roth had returned.

Chapter Three

"Hi, Adam!" Tammy greeted him. Clutching her hands at waist level, she blurted, "Hannah burned the fish."

The tragic tone of her sister's voice made Hannah flush with guilt and embarrassment.

"I could tell from the smell." Adam's expression said he shared in Tammy's sorrow. Then he tossed Hannah a tiny wicked grin. "*And* the smoke. Not much of a cook, are you?"

Hannah just glowered at him, bristling in silence.

Although most of the kitchen windows were open to the summer air, Adam went from one to the other, pushing the sashes up as far as they would go.

"Help me, Tammy," he said. "We need to prop open the front and back doors, too, so this smoke will clear out of the house."

Tammy laughed, eager to help, as she raced to the

living room windows at the front of the house, her grief over the burned fish momentarily forgotten.

Feeling bad that she hadn't paid the frying pan more attention, Hannah heaved a heavy sigh and ended up inhaling enough smoke to make her bend over with a coughing fit.

"Come on," Adam said, taking her by the arm. "Let's step out onto the porch."

Once outside, Hannah grumbled, "I only burned two of the fillets. There's plenty of fish left. It's not like we're going to go hungry."

"Well, it wouldn't matter how much you've got," he commented. "If they're not fit to eat once they're cooked, you just might go hungry."

She didn't want to find the teasing glint in his gray-blue eyes sexy, but she did, as well as the appealing chuckle that rumbled from deep in his chest. Her heart raced; her palms grew clammy. What was the matter with her?

Narrowing her gaze, Hannah put up the best angry front she could. Darn him! Never in a million years would she let this irritating man know she found herself reacting to him, that she found him the least bit attractive. Lord, what was it about this man that made her body react so?

"Why didn't Tammy fry up the fish she caught?" His tone was tinged with accusation.

Hannah made a *tisk* sound to convey the magnitude of her feelings regarding that question. However, before she could speak her mind, Tammy burst onto the back porch. Evidently, the young woman must have heard Adam.

"She likes to take charge," Tammy answered.

"She told me to sit down so she could cook." She shrugged. "So I did." Then she changed the subject completely. "I think I'll go get my fan from my bedroom. It might help blow around some fresh air."

Hannah watched her sister look at Adam, expecting some kind of reply.

He smiled wide. "That's a great idea. You go do that."

Once Hannah was alone with him on the porch again, he turned his gaze her way. His silent query was clearly once again on the matter of the burned fish and why she was cooking rather than Tammy.

She *tisked* again, this time louder.

"Have you seen that monster of a gas stove in there?" She indicated the kitchen. "I had to use a match to light the thing. It must be a hundred years old. And it's dangerous. She can't cook on that thing. It just isn't safe."

"She's been cooking on that monster," Adam replied, "for as long as I've known her." With a raise of his eyebrows, he added, "It's pretty clear to me that she could cook rings around you."

Offended beyond words, Hannah simply stood there mute, a million excuses running around in her head. She was a career woman. A successful nurse in a bustling city hospital. She was a woman of the nineties. A woman who was so competent, so skilled, at her work that she'd soon be the youngest woman ever to be promoted to the ward nurse position.

Who cared if she couldn't cook? Her patients certainly didn't. Neither did her boss *or* her colleagues. And she made enough money to eat out, thank you very much.

However, she didn't voice any of these thoughts, so aggrieved was she at Adam Roth's insult.

"I'll say it again—" His tone was lower when he spoke this time "—you'd better give yourself a chance to get to know Tammy before you race around here changing everything."

Hannah's back teeth began to ache, she was clenching her jaw so tightly against the angry retort hovering on the tip of her tongue.

"What's that picture Tammy's carrying around?" Adam asked her.

Remembering the quandary in which she'd found herself regarding her explanation of who she was to her sister, Hannah couldn't help but wonder if Adam might be able to help. She hated the mere idea of asking him for any kind of guidance, but the man knew Tammy. Hannah had to admit at least that much.

"It's a picture of me," Hannah told him. "When I was six. She doesn't seem to understand who I am."

His bewildered expression urged her to explain further, "I told Tammy I'm her older sister. However, she said I couldn't be Hannah, that her sister was six years old, and then she ran and got that picture as proof. I was about to try to explain to her the concept of growing up when..." She let the sentence trail. "Well, you know what happened."

"You ruined all that wonderful trout."

"I did not ruin *all* of the—" Hannah stopped herself. She didn't need to fight with this man. She didn't have to allow him to gnaw on her last good nerve.

She gave herself time to take a relaxing breath.

"Look," she said, "if you can help me make her understand—"

Just then, Tammy joined them.

"It's clearing up in there," she said, swiping a hand through her glorious golden hair.

"Good," Adam said. "Have you seen Moppet today?"

"Nope," Tammy said. "And I'll bet he's hungry."

She turned and made loud, lip-smacking kissing sounds. "Moppet," she called in a high, singsong voice. "Come here, Moppet."

A fluffy, orange tabby came running from the woods, mewing plaintively. And Hannah recognized it as the one she'd been greeted by earlier today.

Hannah looked at Adam, a silent plea in her own gaze. She'd hoped he would help her explain her identity to her sister, and here he was reminding her to feed her pet cat.

Patience, his gray eyes seemed to tell her, and a complete sense of calm settled over her. It was strange that, with one look, he seemed able to assuage all her doubts and fears.

You, my girl, a small voice chided her, *are giving this man much more credit than he deserves.*

"What a good boy," Tammy crooned, smoothing her hands down the cat's furry back. She stepped inside the door and scooped a cupful of dry cat food from a bag. "Here you go, pretty Moppet." Tammy hummed to the fat cat, petting him as he munched his dinner.

Adam bent down on his haunches next to Tammy, and Hannah's gaze unwittingly darted to his muscular, jeans-clad thighs. She moistened her lips and, tucking her bottom lip between her teeth, forced her eyes back to his handsome face. Back to those gentle steel-blue eyes that made her pulse skip. Damn it! She *would* get over this weird attraction she felt for this man. He was a stranger. A stranger!

"Remember when I first brought Moppet for you?" he asked.

"Yeah," Tammy whispered, smiling. Her tone turned warm with affection. "He was so little. He shivered and shivered, and I wrapped him up in a blanket."

"He did," Adam agreed. "You've taken good care of him. You've fed him and given him a warm, dry place to stay. You've given him lots of love."

"I never forget to take care of Moppet." A deep pride stippled Tammy's words.

"He's grown into a fine fat cat," Adam continued. "Don't you think?"

Tammy nodded, not taking her loving eyes off Moppet.

Ever so gently, he slipped the picture from Tammy's fingers.

"Hannah was a cute little girl," Adam softly observed.

Tammy gazed at him, then at the picture.

Then Adam said, "She's grown up, too."

The young woman's green eyes held a look of momentary confusion. Then she gasped, her gaze flying to her sister. "You *are* Hannah."

Hannah's small nod was accompanied by a tentative smile.

"Adam—" Tammy's tone took on a bubbling excitement "—my sister's come home!"

The young woman fairly sprang at Hannah, the sudden movement making Moppet jump from the porch in fright. Hannah laughed and returned Tammy's tight hug.

"I'm so happy you're here," Tammy said.

Hannah murmured, "I'm happy I'm here, too."

"It's been a long, long time."

Bobbing her head in agreement, Hannah remained silent. She was relieved that Tammy really seemed to understand who she was, although she couldn't imagine her younger sister possessing any memories, seeing she was still a little baby when they had parted.

"I love you." Tammy's eyes glistened warmly. "Gosh, I've loved you forever."

This unrestrained, openhearted expression of emotion made Hannah just a little uncomfortable. She didn't know what to say. She wished she could express a return of Tammy's pure, honest feelings.

However, years had passed since she'd last seen her baby sister. So many years. All during which Hannah had been discouraged from even thinking about Tammy, let alone talking about her. How could Hannah honestly express love for someone who was literally a stranger? She couldn't. At least not with the same unmitigated effusion with which Tammy spoke. So Hannah simply remained silent.

"I'm hungry," Tammy blurted out of the blue. "Are you hungry?"

"Actually, I am," Hannah admitted.

"Why don't you go cook up the rest of that trout?" Adam suggested to Tammy.

"Will you stay for supper?" Tammy asked him. "I'll make my mile-high biscuits."

Hannah felt Adam's questioning gaze on her, and she nodded her reluctant assent. She didn't like the idea of Adam hanging around for dinner, but he had an obvious affection for Tammy, and Hannah felt she might learn more about her from him.

"I'd love to eat supper with you," he told Tammy.

"I'd better get to work, then," Tammy said.

"You'd better," Adam said. "Oh—" he called her back "—I almost forgot." He reached into his pocket. "I brought you this."

He handed her a candy bar.

She sighed a thank-you, then looked at Hannah. "Chocolate. It's my one weakness."

"I don't understand why she simply didn't tell me to get out of her kitchen," Hannah said. "Why did she let me—a complete stranger—come in and just take right over?"

Adam chuckled, a warm, resonating sound that sent tingles coursing across every inch of her skin.

She tried to concentrate on the sound of the songbirds in the trees and the tiny scurrying of what she guessed was a squirrel and the gorgeous clouds streaking mauve across the evening sky as she and Adam walked along the lane while Tammy was back at the house cooking dinner. But it was no use. Adam Roth's presence was simply too formidable for her to ignore. The man made her react in ways she wished she didn't.

"I don't know if anyone's ever told you this before," he murmured, "but you've got a dominating personality."

Her first instinct was to refute what he'd said. But

he was right, she concluded. And she couldn't rail at the man for simply telling the truth.

"I do what I have to," was all she said.

"I'm sure of that."

Hannah wondered what he meant. Was the small comment a compliment or a criticism? Even though she'd only just met this man today, she was pretty sure there was some kind of reproach in what he'd said.

Then he added, "But it's not like Tammy to say absolutely nothing."

His statement was probing, and Hannah found herself thinking back to what had happened in the kitchen before Adam arrived.

"She certainly didn't say anything about wanting to cook," Hannah mused. "All she did was say she was hungry, and she asked if I was, too. In fact, that happened twice, before I decided to make dinner."

"Ah," he said, nodding.

"Ah?" Hannah's brows rose a fraction. "You sound like you understand what happened."

Again he nodded. "I do. You see Tammy understands that...life challenges her in some ways." He smiled and added, "In most ways, actually."

The tender tone of his voice made Hannah's heart warm. He might be irritating at times, but he certainly did treat Tammy with a supreme gentleness.

"She knows," he continued, "that she needs some guidance from the people around her. And that's what she was looking for. A little guidance."

Hannah frowned, putting some of the puzzle pieces together. "Like she sought direction from you regarding her bedroom fan? I thought she was asking permission to bring it down from her room."

Adam shook his head. "No. Not permission, really. She's quite capable of knowing what needs to be done...most of the time." He sighed. "She just wants to know that others agree with her. She needs validation." He shrugged. "Guidance."

Most of the time. The phrase had been slipped in as an aside and seemed innocent enough, but those four small words worried Hannah nonetheless.

"She's very childlike," she observed.

"Tammy is sweet. She's loving and kind. She cares about the people in her life. And we care about her."

Most of the time. The phrase echoed in her head.

"What happens when she makes the wrong assessment of a situation," Hannah asked, "and there's no one around to guide her?"

They walked along the wooded lane for a long while before he spoke. Finally he said, "She gets by. She has up until now. I want you to know that I have every confidence in her. I think she can pretty much take care of herself."

Hannah didn't miss the slight demurral that glazed his words.

"As long as she's got lots of guidance." She felt impelled to add what she was sure must be his unspoken thought.

"Look—" his voice raised a notch along with his chin "—you've got to admit that you have to take Tammy's needs and wants into consideration before you make any decisions about selling her home. She's lived here all her life. It just wouldn't be right for you to up and take Little Haven away from her."

He was spoiling for a fight. But Hannah wasn't going to oblige.

Softly she said, "I'll admit to all of that."

His eyes seemed to turn a deeper blue as relief made them gleam with warmth. "Thank you," he whispered.

The overwhelming heat in the sound of those words, the intensity with which he gazed at her, did something extraordinary to her: she felt it hard to take a breath, her blood turned to fire in her veins and her muscles grew as pliant as warm rubber. Without thought, she reached out and slid her fingers around his taut forearm for support. However, the skin-to-skin contact only aroused her body's reactions all the more.

She wanted to tell him that her admission hadn't altered her plans to sell the house and find a safe place for Tammy to live, it had only put them off until she could spend a little time with her sister. However, Hannah couldn't seem to get her tongue to work properly.

"Are you all right?" There was deep concern etched in the lines on his brow. "You're trembling."

He put his arm about her waist, not realizing that the action only made matters worse for Hannah, not better. With him so near, she felt as if her body were on fire.

"I'm f-fine," she stammered, trying to push herself away from him, away from contact with him.

"Have you eaten today?" he asked.

"No." She could only whisper the words. "At least, not since breakfast."

"You silly woman."

He scooped her up in his arms then, and Hannah murmured a protest. However, he ignored her and started off toward the house.

"Put me down," she ordered. She heard a shakiness in her voice that disgusted her. She didn't care if she had to crawl back, she wouldn't allow herself to be carried when she was perfectly able to—

"Would you just hush," he said. "For once in your life you're going to have to surrender and let someone else dominate the situation."

Hannah came awake slowly the following morning to some out-of-the-ordinary sounds and smells.

The birds that perched in the tree just outside the bedroom window seemed to be in the midst of a family feud, so noisy were they. It wasn't that she hadn't ever heard birds singing, it was just that her apartment was on the twentieth floor, too far above the trees to hear the sounds of New York City's resident fowl. Besides that, she rarely, if ever, even opened her windows, using air-conditioning in the warmer months and the heating system in the cooler ones. So, waking to the frantic chirping was such a different experience that Hannah smiled. She stretched languidly.

Her grin only widened when the rich aroma of just-perked coffee wafted faintly in the air. Tammy must be up.

When Hannah sat up, she frowned and looked down the length of her. Her nightgown was twisted around her body, tight and constricting, as was the cotton sheet. She must have had one fitful night of sleeping.

Supporting herself with one arm, she raked the fingers of the other hand through her mop of tangled hair. Ever so slowly, the wickedly erotic dreams came back to her. Whispery images of skin against skin, lips brushing lips, fingertips sliding sensuously, pulses pounding—and Adam Roth's steel-blue gaze filled with passion as his eyes raked over her body.

"Stop." She murmured the command aloud, throwing back the covers and pushing herself off the mattress.

That man was going to be a big pain in the butt during her days in Little Haven...*and he was going to make her nights a living hell.*

She'd suspected as much yesterday with his warning about Tammy, and then again with his bossy, brutish attitude when he'd picked her up and carried her to the house. But after the way he'd invaded her dreams last night, she knew for certain he was going to be nothing but bad news.

Last night, when she'd found herself—literally—in his arms, a war had waged inside her. She hadn't wanted to enjoy the feel of his hard chest against her cheek, she hadn't wanted to like the clean, warm smell of him, but, darn it, she *had*. And she'd had to stir up a mighty steam of anger to hide all the pleasure she'd found in his nearness.

Luckily Adam hadn't seemed to notice. He'd brought her into the house, plunked her down onto the kitchen chair and started brusquely ordering both Tammy and her about. He didn't seem to settle down until Hannah had eaten and had promised him she no longer felt shaky.

Hannah had decided it was a good thing that Adam had mistakenly blamed her trembling and weakened state on a lack of sustenance. She would have hated for him to realize that it had been her reaction to him that had turned her muscles to jelly.

The man was just too good-looking for words. She didn't need that kind of complication. Not when she had so much to do, so many decisions to make regarding her sister and the estate.

She was going to have to avoid him while she was in Little Haven, that's all there was to it.

Chapter Four

"What do you mean the only person in town who can help me is Adam Roth?" Disappointment rolled over Hannah like a tidal wave as she stood looking at the owner of the town's only hardware store.

The man was short, but looked to be built as solid as a fire hydrant. He shrugged. "Sorry. But this is a small town. We don't have a whole lot to offer by way of professional services."

"I'm not looking for carpentry work," she explained further. "I only want some painting done." She couldn't deny the panic sweeping through her. She didn't want Adam helping her. She didn't want to be anywhere near him. And the idea of seeing him on a day-to-day basis was mind-boggling.

Again, the store owner lifted a beefy shoulder. "Adam's your man. He'll do a great job. Won't cost you an arm and a leg, either."

Was there no way she could avoid the man? Hannah wondered.

She'd decided over her morning coffee that the house needed a good cleaning and a coat of paint. Whatever she decided to do about Tammy—and their father's estate—over the next week or so, she knew she would have to do what she could to make the house more livable...and more salable. Because, in the back of her mind, she was sure that's what would happen in the end.

She hated the idea of approaching Adam for help, but there was no way she could handle this job on her own. Grimacing at the thought, she tried one more tack.

"But aren't there any teenagers looking for a quick buck?" There simply *had* to be someone in this town other than Adam who could wield a paintbrush.

The short, stocky man shook his head. "No one I'd recommend. You should see Adam as soon as possible. Get him to put you on his list."

"His list?"

Reaching up, the man tugged inadvertently on his heavy earlobe. "Adam keeps a list of things to do for people around town. I'm sure he'll get to your paint job as soon as he can."

"Oh, great," Hannah murmured. Not only was she going to have to suffer Adam's presence if she wanted to get her father's house painted, it also looked as if she was going to be at his mercy for when the work would be done.

She heaved a sigh and paid the man for the buckets of paint, the brushes and other various supplies. And as she was loading everything into the trunk of her car, Adam pulled up alongside her in his pickup. She didn't have to look to know it was him; the little hairs that raised up on the back of her neck were warning enough.

"Good morning," he called through the open window.

Hannah tried to suppress the thrill that shot through her when she heard the sound of his voice. What on earth was wrong with her? And what was it about this man that made her react to him so wildly, so unexpectedly?

"It's afternoon," she informed him, inserting a flippancy in her tone that she hoped would conceal her compelling response to him.

His boyish grin only set off more bells and whistles inside her. Her frown deepened.

"So it is," he admitted easily.

Slamming shut the trunk lid, Hannah turned to face him. "I need some painting done on the house," she told him. "I hear you're the only man in town who might be able to help me."

"Oh, I'm sure I can help you."

Was that sexual innuendo she detected in his tone? Her spine straightened, her shoulders squared.

However, before she could voice a cutting rejoinder, he said, "I'd be happy to help you paint the house. But I can't come out today. I'm on my way to take Mr. Andrews to visit his daughter. I take him every Friday afternoon."

"I see." She brushed back her hair and then shielded her eyes from the summer sunlight. "How about tomorrow?"

"I don't work weekends."

One corner of Hannah's mouth pinched tight. "Why doesn't that surprise me?"

Adam chuckled, and her entire body flushed hot at the sexy sound. Her thoughts went haywire, and words failed her.

"I was hoping," he said easily, seemingly unaware of her chaotic plight, "that you'd come fishing with me and Tammy. We'll have fun."

The few seconds that he spoke gave Hannah just enough time to gather her wits about her. She forced a smile onto her lips.

"There's just something about worms and little steel hooks that tells me fishing isn't my kind of sport." She hoped she sounded lighthearted. The last thing she wanted was for this man to realize the discord he caused in her thoughts—*and in her body*—every single time she was near him. "Besides," she continued, "I want to get started on the painting. That house is a mess. Inside and out. And besides that, I still have to go through my father's clothes and personal things."

Adam shrugged. "You know what they say about all work and no play."

"I don't have time to be anything but dull." The sarcastic remark was out of her mouth before she could stop it.

He flashed her another charming grin. "Well, don't blame me when you're an old woman and you regret not experiencing the peace of sitting quietly on the edge of a pond or the feel of a sturdy fishing rod in your palm or perfecting a flawless cast. The whole adventure is like an art form. Nothing else like it to clear the mind." His handsome smile widened. "Or fill the belly."

Ignoring the appeal she was beginning to find in his invitation, Hannah said, "Tammy slipped off this morning and didn't come home for lunch. You don't know where I might find her, do you?"

Adam's blue-gray eyes averted for an instant. Then his shoulders rounded with a shrug. "Why, no. I don't have a clue. But missing one meal isn't going to hurt her."

Was it her imagination, or had his voice raised an octave in volume? And had his words come in an awful rush? Almost as if he was on the defensive. But that's silly, came an immediate response.

"It's not the missed meal I'm worried about," she said. "I told her this morning at breakfast that we need to do a little cleaning. That house isn't fit to live in." Then Hannah chuckled in spite of herself. "Tammy did tell me yesterday that she hates to houseclean, but it wouldn't hurt her to help out just a little. Besides, we have years and years of catching up to do. I'd like to spend some time with her."

He nodded, seeming to understand her reasoning. "If I see her, I'll tell her you're looking for her."

"Thanks."

"Well...I gotta run," he said. "I'll see you later."

"Wait," she called after him, but all she saw was the rear of his truck as he drove away down the street.

Her shoulders sagged. He'd said he didn't work weekends, that he couldn't come tomorrow to paint. But he hadn't told her when he *could* come to start the job. She heaved a sigh. The man continued to be an endless fount of frustration.

* * *

It was early evening before Hannah saw Tammy.

The living room was clean from top to bottom, and Hannah felt gritty and tired. And hungry.

"I've been worried," she said by way of greeting. She tugged the cotton scarf off her head and wiped her forehead with it.

"You don't have to worry about me, Hannah," Tammy said, dumping an armload of fresh vegetables into the sink. "I can take care of myself."

"Honey, I'm not saying you can't." It was only a small lie, Hannah realized. "It would just be nice to know where you are."

Tammy seemed to take offense. "I'm all grown-up."

Hannah looked at her sister. Tammy was twenty-four years old. She'd do well to remember that. However, even though Tammy looked an adult, she had the mind of a child. And Hannah fretted over that. Her sister needed someone to watch over her—constantly—no matter what Adam Roth might think.

"Well," Hannah began, "it's just that..." The thought trickled off. Why did she have such trouble expressing emotions?

"You see," she tried again, "it's only because...I missed you. I was hoping we could spend some time together today...." She moistened her lips. "It's only because I—" again she stammered "—I care about you. That's why I want to know where you go. And what you're doing."

Tammy's clear green eyes glistened with pure joy. "I care about you, too, Hannah."

Warmth filled Hannah's heart, and that heated feeling spilled over and spread into her chest and down her arms.

Then Tammy said, "You look hot. A cool bath might be just what you need."

This time Hannah was able to recognize the tentative tone in her sister's voice. Remembering what Adam told her about Tammy's need for validation, she smiled.

"You know, I think that's a great idea."

Tammy's face just beamed with joy. "I'm hungry. Are you hungry?"

Again Hannah perceived what her sister needed. "Yes, I am. And I hope you're going to do something wonderful with those vegetables."

"Oh, yes," Tammy told her. "I'll steam them with a little butter and lemon juice." Then she looked momentarily panicked. "Or...or I could make a stir-fry."

The query and doubt the young woman was feeling was unmistakable. Hannah reached out and touched Tammy's forearm.

"You make what you like best," she told her. "I'll be happy with whatever you choose."

Tammy's brow smoothed. "You're sure?"

Hannah nodded. "Absolutely. Now I'm going upstairs and take that cool bath just like you suggested."

With a quick, proud smile and a nod, Tammy turned to the sink full of vegetables.

Tammy had been right. A thirty-minute soak in a cool bath had been just what Hannah needed to feel refreshed. Tying the sash of her knee-length satin robe, she went downstairs to see how soon dinner would be ready. She was famished.

Adam was sitting at the kitchen table, and all he offered her by way of a greeting was a slow smile—a slow, *sexy* smile. His cool blue eyes traveled appreciatively down the length of her.

Feeling her whole body react, Hannah lifted her arms and crossed them, as casually as she could, over her breasts. Her nipples budded, her skin tingled. She was relieved that she'd taken a bath, that Adam hadn't arrived to find her dirty and grimy from cleaning.

Not a word was spoken between them; however Hannah felt that they were engaging in an intimate little tête-à-tête. She shouldn't return his smile, shouldn't encourage him in any manner whatsoever, but she could no more have kept her lips from curling up at the corners than she could have stopped a freight train that was steaming along a row of steel tracks.

A sudden stab of self-consciousness forced her gaze to dart to Tammy who was busy at the stove.

"When's dinner?" she asked her sister. "I'm starved."

"The rice will be ready in about five minutes," Tammy said. Then she pointed toward the table. "Adam's here," she announced.

"I see." Hannah's voice softened. "Hi."

"Hi, yourself," he said, as though they hadn't already greeted each other in a silence that could only be described as acute, aware.

Awkwardness descended on her, making her extremely mindful that her legs were bare, as well as her arms and feet. She was by no means naked, but still she felt quite exposed in her thin satin robe.

"Are you two okay?" Tammy asked. "You're not mad at each other, are you?"

Her sister's observation made Hannah feel even more awkward. She let out a discomfited laugh. "Of course we're not angry," she told Tammy. "What would make you think that?"

"Well, you're both awfully quiet."

Again Tammy's perception that something was amiss was like a huge hand that gave Hannah a violent shake. What was she doing, engaging in silent flirtation with Adam? She hadn't even known this man until yesterday. And she'd done nothing but tell herself, again and again, that she didn't have the time or the inclination to do anything except resist stirring up any kind of involvement with him.

"I'm just surprised he's here," Hannah went on, frantically searching for something to say that would somehow diminish the silent eye games she and Adam had just been playing. "When I saw him in town earlier, he said he was too busy to help me out with the painting, too busy giving away his time for free, when he could have been getting ahead, making some money."

Adam got up from the table. "Success and money aren't everything, Hannah. Sometimes people have to come first."

His tone was so soft, she had to strain to hear him. He didn't look insulted or even angry, just a little saddened by what she'd said.

"I only stopped by," he continued, "to make sure Tammy got back safe." His gaze leveled on Tammy. "You need to help Hannah with some housework tomorrow morning," he told her, "*before* you go off...visiting."

Tammy looked at him a moment, then dipped her chin. "Okay, Adam, I will."

Hannah had a fleeting thought that there was something going on between the two of them, her sister and Adam, some unspoken communication to which she wasn't privy. However, she was too stung by the admonishment he'd given her.

Sometimes people have to come first.

The gentle tone of his reprimand only seemed to pack an even more powerful punch than if he'd shouted the words at her.

Is that what he thought? she wondered. That she was too focused on success and money? That she put those things before caring for people? That was ridiculous. She was a nurse. She tended to people every single day. But it didn't hurt to get paid for doing it.

"All I meant..." she began.

Before she could finish, he said, "I know exactly what you meant."

Again she heard a sadness in his voice. A disappointment that was unmistakable.

He moved toward the door, offering Tammy a smile. "I'll say good-night. If you need me, you know where I am."

"I sure do, Adam," Tammy said. "Good night."

Once the door was closed behind him, Hannah felt so empty she hugged her arms about her.

"How come you lied?" Tammy asked.

Surprised, Hannah frowned. "Lied?"

"You said you weren't mad at Adam." Tammy wiped her fingers on the tea towel, her eyes expressing obvious upset. "You were mean to him. You hurt his feelings."

Hannah sighed. "I didn't intend to be mean. I guess I was just irritated that he refused to help me paint the house today, that he'd choose to take some man to visit his daughter rather than earn a few dollars. I mean, why couldn't the man's daughter come and visit him?"

She wasn't really expecting an answer to her question. She was just babbling, really. Trying to cover up the fact that it hadn't really been Adam's refusal to help her today that had her so agitated, it was his mere presence that did it.

"Mr. Andrews's daughter can't come visit him, silly," Tammy said. "Adam takes Mr. Andrews to the graveyard to tend his family plot. She's buried in the same cemetery as Daddy."

Embarrassment and regret plowed into Hannah like a ten-ton truck moving at sixty miles an hour. Her arms dropped to her sides. The urge to go and apologize to him blindsided her. She felt a desperate need to tell him she hadn't known the whole story behind his trip with Mr. Andrews. That she shouldn't have said the things she had.

No! logic spoke loud and clear. *Don't you move an inch from this spot! Let him think the worst of you. What do you care, anyway? If he thinks you're an awful, uncaring person, then there will be no more silent, flirty games played between you.*

There was sound reasoning behind the thought, but it wasn't enough to keep her feet from running across the floor, or her hand from reaching out, turning the knob and shoving open the back door.

"Adam," she called before she was even out onto the porch.

He was getting into his pickup. He paused and then turned to face her in the dusky evening.

Lord, he looked so good standing there in the twilight. He looked strong and safe and secure.

All of her life she'd never had need of these things from someone else, she'd always relied completely on her own abilities to succeed and survive. So she had no idea why these things—why *he*—appealed to her so very much.

The grass felt cool against her bare feet as she trotted across the yard. She expected to feel panic well up in her. Expected questions to flood her mind regarding what she would say to him, how she should explain her behavior. But she didn't experience any of that.

"I'm sorry." The simple words seemed right.

His heavy brows drew together. "You don't have to apologize, Hannah."

"But I do," she said. "I didn't know the whole story about you…your helping Mr. Andrews. About your taking him to the cemetery. Tammy just told me. I was too quick to judge. Too quick to make an assumption of the situation. It's good, what you do for that old man. Very caring, very good. And I had no right to diminish your act of kindness."

Adam closed the truck door, never taking his eyes from her face. He lifted his hand, slowly stroking the pads of his fingers over his chin, once, twice, three times, as he obviously contemplated how he should respond.

Finally he said, "You surprise me, Hannah Cavanaugh."

The summer air was still and quiet. She waited, breathless, for him to elaborate.

He rubbed his palm against the back of his head, and then his arms dropped to his sides.

"I thought I knew you." His voice was as soft as the approaching nightfall. "I had you pegged as one of those women who was so focused on getting what she wanted, and getting it quickly, that she took no notice of anything or anyone around her."

Many moments passed in silence. Hannah didn't know what was taking place between her and Adam. They didn't touch. Didn't speak. But she felt somehow closer to him. That this man she barely knew had suddenly become important to her. And for the life of her, she couldn't figure out why.

Then he smiled in the waning light, and Hannah's heart *ka-chunked* in her chest.

"I'm coming to the conclusion," he said, "that I may have been mistaken."

He got into his truck, then he started the engine and, after giving her one more long, intense look, he drove away.

Her hunger forgotten, Hannah stood there until his taillights disappeared through the trees, until all that was left were the sounds of the night, the chirping of the crickets, the croaking of the frogs. And even then she remained riveted to the spot, her gaze staring down the narrow dirt lane that led to the main road.

What was happening to her? What was this heated magnetism she felt when she was near Adam? When she simply *thought* of him?

She had no answers. None at all.

The weekend passed, slow but sure. Hannah used the days to give the rest of the house a good cleaning. She washed curtains, shook out throw rugs, dusted baseboards, scrubbed floors, shined windows. She doubted the rooms had received this kind of attention in a good, long while. Tammy helped with the chores. Not joyously or even willingly, Hannah smiled to remember, but her sister lent a hand nonetheless.

Late Sunday evening she and Tammy had gone through their father's clothes. They'd folded up the few trousers and shirts, belts and shoes and packed them into large plastic bags so that Hannah could take them to a homeless shelter. Tammy had been very subdued as they'd emptied the chest of drawers, but Hannah had gently cajoled her sister into talking about the man with whom she'd lived all her life.

Tammy had only had good things to say about Bobby Ray. He was loving and generous. It was obvious that she felt her daddy had kept her safe and loved her no matter what kind of "problems" she might have been born with.

This intimation had surprised Hannah. Adam had told her that Tammy knew she was challenged, but this was the first hint that her sister had given Hannah of the obstacles she faced every single day.

When Hannah had inquired after Bobby Ray's occupation, Tammy had been a little vague. It seemed that their father had worked here and there. Odd jobs that never lasted long and, from what Tammy said, were few and far between. Finally Hannah had come right out and asked her sister how her father had paid the bills for the utilities: the electric, the telephone and the gas for cooking and heating. Tammy had become animated for the first time since they'd gone into their father's room.

"Oh, you don't have to worry about that," Tammy had said. "Our state checks pay for the bills."

"Checks?" she'd asked. "You get more than one?"

"I get one," Tammy had told her, "and Daddy gets one." She paused, then sadly corrected, "Well, he used to get one, anyway."

Hannah realized then that she'd have to contact the state agencies that were sending the money that her sister and father lived on. She surmised that Tammy's funds came from the board of health, or whatever agency dealt with people who couldn't provide for themselves due to a mental handicap. Her father's check, she suspected, must come from the state welfare office.

Sadly, Hannah had come to the silent conclusion that her mother had been right about Bobby Ray. He hadn't had much ambition, and success wasn't important to him. But even though it looked as if the man had been a ne'er-do-well who couldn't hold down a job, Hannah would still have loved to have had the opportunity to know him. When all was said and done, no matter what kind of provider he'd turned out to have been, he'd still been her father.

Now it was close to noon on Monday, and Hannah had spent the past three hours scraping dried, curling paint chips from posts on the front porch. It was backbreaking work, but it had to be done before she could begin applying a fresh coat of white paint. Hannah grinned as she thought of the slight disagreement she and Tammy had had over the color of the paint. Tammy had wanted pink, she'd said, and she'd boldly complained about not being consulted before the supplies had been purchased. But Hannah had calmed her, explaining that white was a much better color for a Victorian house such as theirs, and Tammy had sullenly acquiesced. In reality, Hannah knew a neutral color would make the house much more appealing to a buyer.

Just as he'd said he'd planned, Adam had gone off fishing with Tammy over the weekend. However, he'd made Hannah very happy by telling her he would try to come sometime at the beginning of this week to start painting the house. So—now that it was the beginning of this week—she was trying to complete some of the prep work so they could begin painting just as soon as he arrived.

When she'd seen him this weekend, the air had hummed with a low, vibrating current. Her gaze kept darting to his, and he'd blessed her, again and again, with his sexy smile. Lord, her whole body had come alive.

Just thinking about him now made her mouth go dry with desire.

Yes, desire!

That's exactly what it was that she'd been feeling for this man. A deep, soulful yearning that caused her breath to catch and her heart to race. It had taken her days to identify what was happening to her since meeting him, and now she knew.

She wasn't sure how she felt about it. In fact, she had tried not to think about it at all. However, thoughts of Adam were not easy to dissuade. His hands were so strong, but they could also be gentle. She knew this from experience. And she could still feel the hardness of his chest as he'd carried her in his arms—

Just then Tammy slipped around the corner of the house, stealthy and quiet. Hannah would have missed seeing her altogether if she hadn't seen a flash of yellow from her sister's pretty dress in the periphery of her vision.

"Tammy," she called, climbing down a rung or two from the rickety step ladder.

"I'll be back really soon, Hannah." The young woman kept walking away from the house, her gait so quick it could almost have been described as a jog.

"Wait a second, honey. I want to talk to you." When her sister showed no signs of slowing, Hannah called out sharply, "Tammy!"

There was reluctance and frustration in Tammy's face as she turned and made her way back toward the porch.

"Hannah, I made my bed and I washed the breakfast dishes just like you asked. I want to go into town."

"Okay," Hannah said, descending the ladder and brushing at the little chips of paint in her hair and on her clothes. "But I need to talk to you about something first."

Tammy's shoulders slumped, and Hannah nearly laughed. It was so obvious that her sister thought she was going to be asked to do more of those dratted housecleaning chores.

"I wanted to ask you about the car," Hannah said,

looking over at the rusty automobile that was parked at the very edge of the yard. She had no idea if it even ran, but she knew she'd have to get rid of it somehow.

Taking a slow step closer, Tammy's gaze narrowed as she asked, "What about the car?"

"I was thinking that I should advertise it in the local paper," Hannah said. "It probably isn't worth more than a hundred dollars or so, but with Dad gone, we really don't need it."

"Advertise it in the paper?" Tammy's porcelain skin was marred with a confused frown.

"Yes," Hannah said. "I'd like to sell it. Get that rusty bucket of bolts out of the yard. What do you think?"

Tammy stood there, her confusion turning to understanding, her understanding turning to wide-eyed panic. Before Hannah had a chance to speak, her sister flew up the steps past her into the front door of the house. She hadn't been gone long enough for Hannah's chaotic thoughts to clear before she burst back out through the screen door, car keys jingling in her hand, anger burning in her eyes.

"You can come marching in here and take over all you like," Tammy shouted. "You can burn up all the trout I catch. You can pack up all my daddy's clothes and give them away. And you can paint this house any boring color you want. But I won't—" she actually stomped her foot childishly on the wooden planks of the porch floor "—I *won't* let you take away my fun times!"

Tammy ran down the steps and raced across the yard.

"Wait!" Hannah called, guilt and fear and confusion setting in over having upset her sister to this degree. "Tammy, please wait."

But her sister couldn't be stopped. She tugged open the rusty car door, got inside and revved up the engine. The car coughed and sputtered, and in a flash, Tammy shoved it into gear.

And while Hannah looked on, horrified and unable to move, the young woman drove off into the thick cover of the trees, leaving behind a tail of blue exhaust hovering in the hot summer air.

Chapter Five

Hannah was frantic. She watched the blue haze of car exhaust rise...and thin...and then vanish altogether, and still her thoughts were too frenzied for her to latch on to anything calm and logical enough to be called a solution or a course of action.

"Stop," she murmured to herself, commanding her thoughts to cease their torturous churning.

This helpless feeling was so alien to her. She worked in the medical profession. She faced dangerous and life-threatening emergencies almost daily at the hospital. Still...this was Tammy who had just driven off in two tons of rusty, squeaking steel. This was her baby sister who was at risk.

Somehow that made all the difference in the world.

Should she follow Tammy?

Hannah looked at her small compact and then back at the dirt trail through the trees where Tammy had disappeared. She shook her head. Her car would never survive an excursion through those woods.

The police? The fire company? She considered dialing 911, but quickly dismissed the idea. The situation wasn't *that* critical, she decided. No one was hurt. Yet.

The tiny word set her thoughts racing again.

Oh, Lord, she needed to go after Tammy. She ran inside to grab her keys, even though she knew her flimsy little car wouldn't be able to handle the dips and bumps of the rough track. The trail through the woods looked even more rutted than the lane leading from the house to the main road.

The keys on the ring cut into her palm as she grasped them. What she needed was one of those fancy, four-wheel-drive vehicles. No, what she needed was a pickup truck.

Adam.

She needed Adam.

The ring of keys clattered to the kitchen floor, forgotten, as she reached for the phone.

Adam pressed the gas pedal to the floor as he drove the short distance to Bobby Ray's house. He shook his head. The house belonged to Tammy now. Tammy and Hannah, he corrected yet again.

Hannah had been so upset on the telephone that he'd barely been able to understand a word she'd said. All he'd heard through her babbling was that Tammy was gone and that he must come—now!

Tires squealed in protest as he turned down the dirt lane that led to the Cavanaughs'. *That lead to Hannah.*

His heart raced with fear, yet the echoing thought was enough to give him pause, to make him blink with utter surprise.

Where had *that* idea come from?

Ever since Bobby Ray had died all those weeks ago, Adam had done what he could for Tammy. He'd checked on her daily to see that she ate properly, to see that she took care of herself. And so far he'd succeeded in doing it in a manner that hadn't offended her, that hadn't made her feel in any way belittled. He'd seen to it that her checks from the state would continue to arrive. And right after Bobby Ray's funeral he'd gotten together with Little Haven's only lawyer, Hank Tillis, to contact Tammy's next of kin.

So why was it, now that he'd discovered Tammy might be in trouble, that his first thought was for *Hannah?* The high-handed, barge-in-and-take-over woman who had irritated the daylights out of him from the first day he'd laid eyes on her?

That's a lie, Adam, a silent voice raised up in his brain. *A bold-faced lie.*

She hasn't irritated you. She's tempted you. With her strawberry-blond hair swinging and her green eyes flashing. Oh, how she's tempted you. And that's what you've found irritating.

"Ah, shut up," he grumbled, bringing his truck to a sliding halt and shoving the gearshift into park.

Hannah was out the front door and down the porch steps before he had time to shut the door of his truck.

"Get back in! We have to go after her."

Her beautiful jewel-green eyes were wide and wild. Adam caught her arm, feeling a terrible need to calm her.

"Wait," he said softly.

She slapped at his hands, fighting off his touch.

"She's *driving*. The *car*. She's going to hurt herself. We've got to go after her. Now!"

The frantic quality in her tone and the worried frown biting cruelly into her brow just about broke his heart.

"I said wait." He firmed his hold on her arm. Not enough to hurt, only to make her stop and listen to him.

And that's exactly what she did.

He focused his gaze on her intently, like she was the only thing in existence. "I need you to calm down and tell me what happened."

There were a dozen separate thoughts running through Hannah's mind; he could see that. And he knew she wouldn't be any good to Tammy until she'd regained her composure.

"I was scraping paint chips," she began. "From the porch. I saw Tammy leaving. Just like everyday. But I stopped her. I asked her about Dad's car. Told her I thought we should sell it. A-and she flipped out. She ran in and snatched up the keys. Then she proceeded to pretty much tell me off. How bossy I've been. And then she declared she wouldn't let me take away the car. No. She said her *fun times*. She wouldn't let me take away her fun times. Then she raced to the car, got in and drove off into the woods. I haven't seen her since."

She looked so vulnerable and frightened that he wanted to hug her to him.

"I was going to follow her," she continued, "but

I knew my car would never survive the trip. Then I thought of you."

His chest swelled with pleasure and pride when he heard that he was the one she'd thought of in times of trouble. His very first impression of this woman had been that she was independent and self-sufficient to a fault, but he was discovering every day that she wasn't like that at all. She was soft and needy, just like a woman ought to—

"I thought of your *truck*," she amended. "It's just what I need to go out on that dirt trail after her."

His gaze widened, and then he blinked, feeling like an overblown balloon that had been pricked with a sharp pin.

"We really need to go after her."

Several silent seconds ticked.

"Come on, Adam!"

He didn't let go of her arm, and even though she'd stomped on his feelings like they were dirt under her feet, he still felt that alleviating her fear about Tammy's safety was the decent thing to do.

"She's fine," he told Hannah.

Irritation flared in her green eyes. "How can you say that? *She drove off in Dad's car.* She's out there now swerving around trees and bushes and into gullies and who knows what else. We've got to find her. Get her out of that car."

He firmly repeated, "She's fine."

Hannah searched his face.

"It's *her* car," he went on. "Not Bobby Ray's."

"What do you mean? That's impossible. The state wouldn't give her a license."

"You're right," he explained. "The state didn't.

But the car isn't tagged for road use. It's like a piece of farm equipment. Or a riding lawn mower. She doesn't need a license as long as she stays on her property. And that's exactly what she does."

Hannah was silent a moment, taking it all in. Then she said, "And this was okay with Bobby Ray? And you?"

He gave a tiny shrug. "Sure. Why wouldn't it be?"

Her gaze narrowed. "Because a riding mower can't reach speeds of sixty or seventy miles an hour. Tammy is not safe driving around in that car."

He pressed his lips together, his own annoyance stirred now. "Hannah, I've been telling you over and over that Tammy is pretty darn capable. But you keep refusing to listen to me. She's been driving that car—having her fun times—for years now. *Years.* You think that should change simply because you've come into town?" He paused, hoping the idea would sink into Hannah's brain. "Not once has she wrecked the car or hurt herself or anyone else. Not once has she driven off the trail. Not once has she left the property. She knows right from wrong. And she's competent enough to go on driving that car."

He frowned. "She deserves a life. A life full of challenge, full of pushing the limits, full of enjoyment, full of *fun times.*" He shook his head in sad amazement. "How could you want anything less for her?"

Suddenly Hannah's shoulders slumped a fraction and she looked off toward the dense woods.

"You promise she's okay?" she whispered.

Hannah's concern for Tammy melted every bit of aggravation he'd felt toward her.

"I promise." He smiled even though she wasn't looking at him. "She'll be back before too long. You'll see."

She inhaled deeply, her gaze swinging back to his face. "Tammy was so upset with me. She accused me of taking over. I know she's right. I did force my way right into her life."

Her tone had become whispery and much less assured, and Adam felt an overwhelming urge to comfort her. But he didn't move a muscle, just continued to listen.

"But it was only because I thought she needed it," she continued. "I only meant to help."

Guilt glistened in her eyes, and Adam's heart clenched painfully. He reached up and stroked her cheek, his chest aching with a deep compassion.

She heaved a soulful sigh and then looked up into his face. "Thanks for coming so quickly. I don't know what I'd have done without you." Her snicker was humorless and she averted her gaze. "I'd have gone crazy, I guess," she murmured.

Then her green eyes fluttered up to meet his once again. "Thanks, Adam," she said. "I mean it."

"Anytime."

He hadn't meant to put a flirtatious inflection on his response, however, that tiny little adverb seemed to light a spark between them. The air seemed to still, grow heavy. He tried hard to hold back the words hovering on his tongue. He failed.

"I mean it."

The spark flared into flame. White-hot flame.

Their gazes locked and held, and he truly felt there was nothing else in the world but her and him. She felt the sensuous isolation, he could read it in her eyes. He lowered his head, and at the same time she rose up onto her toes. Somewhere in the heated space between, their lips met.

She tasted of wild honey. Of fresh spring rain. And the smell of her filled his nostrils, arousing his desire, taking his emotions up a notch higher. His fingers dived into her thick, silky hair and he pulled her to him tightly.

He felt the heat of her fingertips on his jaw, his cheek and then the back of his neck as she, too, tugged him close, closer. It was like they were starved, hungry for this soul-searing kiss. Like they had both been waiting for it all their lives.

The invisible current whipping around them made his head swim. He felt disoriented and dizzy. The out-of-control feeling might have confounded another man, but he loved it. Reveled in it. Wanted to get lost in it.

Sliding his lips from hers, he kissed her cheekbone, her ear, her neck. She tasted sweet and soft. His heart hitched in his chest when she groaned, and the yearning deep in his gut blistered and sizzled until he, too, was forced to gasp from the sheer heat of it.

He whispered her name, pulling back just enough to look into her passion-filled eyes.

"What *is* this?" she murmured. "What's happening?"

"I don't know," he told her ever so softly. "But I've felt it since the first time we met."

She gently dragged her fingernails up the side of his neck, causing a delicious shiver to course down his spine. The velvety pads of her fingers felt like heaven as she trailed them along the line of his jaw.

He wanted to hear her say she had felt the attraction, too. That she'd been aware of the humming vibration that always seemed to surround them. *Connect them.*

"I can't do this," she said. "I just can't."

But even as she murmured the words, she pulled him to her again. And Adam allowed himself to be led.

Her mouth was hot and moist and aggressive against his, her tongue tasting him, her teeth nipping. Adam closed his eyes and enjoyed her ardent invasion.

Another groan escaped from deep in her throat, and Adam didn't think he could hold on to sanity much longer. Her short, forceful exhalation was hot against his skin.

Again she whispered, "I can't do this."

Again she crushed her mouth to his.

For something she kept proclaiming she couldn't do, she was certainly relishing the doing. So was Adam.

Afraid that her brain would actually connect with the words spilling from her lips and that she'd pull away from him, he slid his arms securely around her body.

She felt so good. So near. With her luscious breasts pressed tight against him. The heat of her, radiating like rays from the summer sun, warming him. He didn't want to let her go. Ever.

The next time she leaned her head back a fraction,

he saw that her lips were puffy and moist. The sight nearly sent him over the edge.

"I can't do this," she whispered, yet again. "I want to. But I just can't."

He couldn't bring himself to ask why. He didn't want to know. Didn't want to be bothered with complications. All he wanted to do was continue tasting her, touching her. Continue feeling the touch of her skin on his.

She reached out for him again, and it was then that her hip bone pressed up against the hardness of his desire.

Her eyes went wide, her breath catching in a gasp, and her hands stilled. Then she planted her palms on his shoulders and pushed away from him.

"I have to stop this, Adam. I'm sorry, but I have to stop."

She swallowed, his attention riveted to the delicate convulsing motion along the length of her milky throat. Just a moment ago he'd kissed the heated, silky spot, he'd felt her pulse beating thick and heavy just under her skin.

He closed his eyes, raking his fingers through his hair.

Panic glazed her voice as she said, "I can't let this happen again. I can't give in to...to..." Her words trailed off as she failed to find the right noun to describe what was happening to them. "I have too much to do. And not enough time in which to do it. I can't let things get...tangled up. I just can't...get involved."

Adam leaned against the fender of his truck, using every ounce of strength in him to rein in his runaway libido. He wanted this woman. And she wanted him. Nothing in his life had ever been more certain to him.

However, if she refused to surrender to what was happening between them, if she declined to submit to the desires she clearly felt, then there was absolutely nothing he could do about it.

Nothing.

An acidic bitterness, sharp and sour, welled up inside him. And he realized the feeling was fueled by the deep hunger he felt for her—the deep hunger she'd just turned her back on.

She didn't have to tell him her reason for refusing to act on what she felt for him. He knew why.

Her career. Her big, important job in that big, important hospital up north. She already had a life in New York City. A life that didn't have room in it for him or anything he might be able to offer her.

Hannah was determined to reject him for her occupation. She was willing to forego anything that they might have experienced together just so her perfect life wouldn't be altered. Just as she was determined to jerk Tammy away from everything that was familiar, from everyone who cared about the young woman. All for her own selfish wants and desires, her own selfish goals.

Maybe she wasn't so unlike the women he'd met in his past, after all.

Tammy didn't show up for twenty minutes—twenty *long, awkward* minutes. And during every single one of them, Hannah had been unable to look at Adam, let alone speak to him.

Why in the world had she allowed herself to act so rashly? So carelessly? *So wantonly?*

The last revealing question caused her face to flame with embarrassment, and she walked a dozen or so paces away from him, away from the unpleasant silence that had hovered and then settled, so unceremoniously, between them.

At last the sound of the car engine could be heard through the trees. Hannah stopped her pacing. Tammy emerged from the woods, and Hannah could see her sister's beaming smile through the windshield. The sigh that passed her lips was one of complete relief that Tammy was safe and sound.

Adam had promised Tammy's safe return, Hannah remembered, and she'd been terribly grateful for his comforting words. However, there was nothing like actually seeing her sister arrive unharmed.

Tammy parked the car exactly in the spot from which she'd taken it. Her smile as she came toward them was broad and carefree.

"Driving that car is so fun," Tammy said joyously. She grinned at Hannah. "It's my one weakness." She looked over at Adam. "I just can't get enough of it."

Hannah was amazed that there didn't seem to be an ounce of discernable malice in Tammy. It was as if their argument had never happened. However, simply because Tammy had let go of all the bad emotions she'd been feeling didn't mean that Hannah shouldn't deal with them.

"Tammy," Hannah said, "I want to apologize."

Her sister's innocent green gaze focused on her and her smile faltered. Hannah knew Tammy understood what she was talking about.

"I didn't know the car belonged to you," she continued. "I didn't know you were the one who drove it. I'm sorry that I made the assumption that it belonged to Bobby—" she stopped herself "—to our dad."

Sympathy softened Tammy's expression. "That's okay, Hannah. Everybody makes mistakes now and then." She looked at Adam. "Isn't that right, Adam?"

He nodded. "That's exactly right."

"We won't sell the car," Hannah told her. "At least, not now. We'll wait."

Until we have to leave for New York, the thought finished silently in her head. But something kept her from uttering it.

Tammy reacted to the news with childlike delight.

Why had she hesitated in telling Tammy the full truth? Hannah wondered. What had kept her from explaining her plans to sell the house and the surrounding property? Her intention of moving her sister to the city to be near her?

It wasn't that she *couldn't* tell Tammy, Hannah decided. It was that this simply wasn't a good time. Not after Tammy had been so upset by the car. She'd have to wait, choose the timing carefully—

Hannah found herself wrapped in Tammy's warm embrace.

"I'm so happy, Hannah," Tammy said. "Let's go for a ride. Right now. Me and you—" Tammy turned to look at Adam "—and Adam. Will you come?"

Shaking her head, Hannah said, "Oh, but I don't think—"

"I'd love to!"

Hannah tossed Adam a withering look.

"Come on, Hannah," he cajoled. "It'll be fun."

The softly spoken words were the first he'd voiced to her since the searing kisses they had shared. The mere sound of his voice was enough to have her averting her gaze.

Tammy was bouncing on the balls of her feet, her expression gleeful and grinning. How could Hannah refuse?

Smiling at her sister, Hannah lifted her palms up and then gave her thighs an acquiescing slap. "Okay," she said. "Let's go."

Racing toward the car, Tammy laughed, and Hannah couldn't help but get caught up in the infectious quality of it. Apparently, neither could Adam.

His grin was enough to charm the clouds from the sky.

"You're not going to regret this," he told her.

"I'll reserve my opinion," Hannah remarked, "until I get out of the car with all my limbs intact."

Adam chuckled. "Oh, we'll be fine."

Hannah did notice that her agreeing to take the joy ride had lessened the awkward air between herself and Adam.

She slid into the front seat and was surprised when Adam climbed in right behind her. Scooting over next to her sister, Hannah felt the heat of Adam's body pressed up against her shoulder and hip.

Tammy's seat belt clicked as she latched together the two ends. Hannah reached for her belt, as did Adam. The two fabric strips might not offer total security, Hannah thought, but she was going to take full advantage of what little confidence and peace of mind the belt could give.

Adam grinned at her. "Hang on. Here we go."

The engine revved when Tammy pressed the accelerator, and Hannah's hands automatically flew to the dashboard for support as the car shot forward.

Tree branches brushed the roof, and bramble bushes scratched at the doors as they careered down the bumpy trail through the woods. The path wound and twisted back on itself, then turned yet again to lead them to an open meadow.

Tammy didn't drive all that fast, Hannah realized, twenty or twenty-five miles per hour at most. Still, each curve tossed her against Adam, until he finally drew his arm across the back of her shoulders to lend her some support during the wild ride.

"We're having some fun times now!" Adam said.

Hannah's fear faded, and she joined in with laughter. She couldn't help it—she was actually enjoying herself.

"That's exactly what Daddy used to say," Tammy cried.

Warm sentiment pinched at Hannah's heart. Now she knew what her sister had meant when she'd refused to allow Hannah to take away her "fun times."

Hannah glanced up at Adam, and the look glittering in his eyes told her that he'd purposefully repeated Bobby Ray's words for Tammy's benefit. This man really and truly cared about her sister. It was evident in the way he treated Tammy, in the manner he talked to her, in the things he did for her.

Her emotions regarding Adam Roth twisted into a confused mass. He made her feel things she didn't want to feel. Made her react in ways she didn't want to react.

Just then, Adam shouted out encouragement as Tammy steered the car into a large circle and they went round and round. Centrifugal force pushed Hannah against Adam's muscular chest, and she could hear the deep rumble of his laughter close to her ear. Silky. Sexy. Delectably tempting.

The world spun, and a carefree laugh slipped from her lips.

Again the car shot through the trees, and before she knew it, they were once more parked near the house.

Hannah grinned at her sister. "I've never had so much fun in my whole life." And as she thought about it, she realized it was the absolute truth.

"It is fun, isn't it?" Tammy took the keys from the ignition and got out of the car.

After unlatching her seat belt, Hannah went to exit the car as well. However, Adam sat in her way, seeming not the least interested in getting out just yet.

His gray-blue eyes were trained on her. And he reached up and gave her cheek a feathery stroke. Then he whispered, "You ought to do more things for the pure fun of it."

Chapter Six

Hannah's fierce grip on the steering wheel turned her knuckles white as she drove through the town of Little Haven. She was furious. And as soon as she found Adam, she fully intended to tell him exactly what she thought of him and his sneaky, underhanded ways.

Ever since their ride in the car with Tammy three days ago, it seemed that the relationship between Hannah and Adam had...changed. The air between them remained tense. It snapped and sparked, and she was in a constant state of acute self-consciousness. Utter awareness, not in the least subliminal but terribly supraliminal, pervaded her being when she was anywhere near the man.

Ever since that darned car ride—

Who do you think you're kidding? a snide inner voice taunted her. *What's happening between you and*

Adam has nothing whatsoever to do with the ride in Tammy's car. It was that kiss!

She had lost control of herself with Adam, and she was still kicking herself about her behavior.

The disdainful voice piped up again, *Your guilt over that kiss is what's fueling your fury against him now.*

"It is not," Hannah said aloud to the empty car. "That man told Tammy to lie to me. He encouraged her to be deceptive. And I just found out about it this morning. He deserves every bit of anger I'm feeling. Every bit."

When she'd found Tammy with...

Hannah smoldered, pushing the memory aside. She didn't want to dwell on the incident. She wanted to save up every ounce of her wrath so she could level it on the guilty party—Adam. How could he condone such a thing?

Hannah had already inquired after Adam's whereabouts at the doughnut shop on Main Street. The woman there had directed her to the hardware store. The man there told Hannah that Adam was doing some work for a lady on Walter Street.

Turning down the tree-lined roadway, she saw his truck parked in front of a small bungalow. She pulled up behind his vehicle and got out of her car.

Before she had even stepped up onto the sidewalk, she saw him working in the garden out in the backyard.

"Adam!" she called from the chain-link fence that bordered the property.

He gazed up at her.

Before he had time to even smile at her she declared, "I want to talk to you."

She hurled the words like they were tiny stones, wanting their impact to be felt. He needed to know up-front that this wasn't a pleasure visit.

Adam stood up and brushed the soil from the knees of his trousers. There was a resigned set to his mouth as he came toward her.

Heavens, Hannah thought as she watched him saunter across the grass, he looks so darned good. His gray-blue eyes were such a contrast to his raven-wing hair and his tanned complexion. He was a startlingly handsome man.

Stop. She nearly murmured the word aloud.

It didn't matter how good-looking he was. He'd plotted and planned with Tammy to deceive her. And she wouldn't stand for that.

"Good afternoon, Hannah," he said.

"There's nothing good about it."

He reached out and unlatched the gate. "Why does it not surprise me to hear you say that?"

Rather than usher her into the yard, as she'd expected him to do, he stepped out onto the sidewalk, took her by the arm and steered her down the street.

His touch was enough to send her senses reeling. Hannah was disconcerted by how the mere warmth of him could make her heart palpitate. They had traveled several feet before she asked, "What are you doing? Where are we going?"

"You obviously have something on your mind," he surmised, his tone lowering. "Something you'd like to discuss. I think it would be best if we tried to find a little privacy."

Looking over her shoulder, Hannah saw the elderly woman who sat on the porch of the little bungalow, her dark-tinted glasses and red-and-white striped cane alerting the world to her blindness.

"I'll be back in a bit, Mrs. Blake," Adam called out to the woman, and he received a wave in response.

Hannah and Adam walked several more yards before he spoke. When he evidently thought they were out of hearing distance, he said, "She knows everything about everyone in this town. And there's a good reason for that."

Frowning, Hannah waited for him to elaborate.

"Gossip," was all he said. Then one corner of his mouth cocked upward. "Not that gossiping is a bad thing, in and of itself. It gives Mrs. Blake something to do with her time, and being privy to information has even come in handy for me a time or two. However, I don't care to be the topic of Little Haven conversation. And I don't expect you do, either."

Unable to bring herself to tell him his conjecture was correct, Hannah simply remained mute as they walked down the street together.

Adam chuckled. "Although Mrs. Blake is sure to put her own spin on why the new girl in town was so anxious to pull me away from my work."

There was a hint of eroticism in his words, a dark and mysterious sensuality that made Hannah gasp.

"She wouldn't think such a thing," she said, horrified. "Would she?"

He shrugged. "I *am* the town's most eligible bachelor."

His stormy gray eyes were troubled and tense when he leveled his gaze on her. "Tammy and Brian are in love. But you have to understand that their affection for one another is very...innocent."

"You can't be serious." Hannah looked away, overwhelmed by the only word she heard—love. "Please tell me that you do not support the idea of my sister being involved in any kind of serious relationship."

His silence answered her question.

"Adam..." Her thought petered out as she shook her head. She tried again. "My sister might be twenty-four, but she's got the mental capacity of a teenager. And you said it yourself, that young man that you're claiming Tammy's in love with has some challenges of his own. You cannot think—" She bit her lip. "They simply aren't able to make the right decisions. What if—"

A solid wall of pure panic broadsided her as she thought of all the problems and complications such a relationship could bring.

"We cannot allow this to continue." Every muscle in her body felt rigid.

Adam leaned against the back of the bench as he reached up, absently pinching his chin between his index finger and thumb. Dark thoughts were whirling around in his head. Hannah couldn't guess what they were, but she knew she was about to find out.

"Are you trying to tell me that you believe," he said, "that simply because two human beings happen to be mentally challenged that they don't deserve to experience love?"

His question was a loaded one, and Hannah had no

intention of debating an issue as ocean-deep as this. Her only design was doing what she thought was best for Tammy.

"This problem," she said, "is much more complicated than that—"

"Or could it be," he went on, overriding her retort, "that your aversion to Tammy's romantic involvement with Brian has less to do with your sister's mental state and more to do with the fact that your sister has a man in her life."

"What are you talking about?" Hannah's shoulders squared, her spine stiffening.

"You with your all-important job up north," he said. "You're an independent woman who resents any female who wants to depend on a man."

"That's ridiculous!" she blurted out.

She went suddenly quiet. What he'd said wasn't all that absurd. Why should she cover the truth? she wondered. He *was* off the mark when he said she was resentful. However, she had always prided herself on being self-reliant. It wasn't wrong that she would want the same for her sister. So why did his comment have her feeling so indignant? Why did his allegation provoke her?

Because, although Adam had espoused her fundamental principle and belief, he'd also succeeded in making it sound somehow...flawed. Like there was something wrong with her life philosophy.

She hopped up from the bench. "I'm not going to sit here," she said, "and allow you to play armchair psychologist. You are the last person I want delving into my psyche."

The pine needles under her feet were soft and pliant

as she turned to leave, but something made her swing back around.

"When the heck are you coming to paint my house?" she asked. "You promised me you'd come early in the week. Well, it's now Thursday. Where I come from, Thursday comes at the end of the week."

His eyes had turned to slate, his forehead creased with tension. As Hannah looked at him, she realized it felt good to inform him that he'd broken his word, that he'd let her down. And she wondered if that conquering feeling was necessary because he'd so successfully smacked her in the face with her own convictions.

"Mrs. Blake's garden is the last job on my list," he told her, his tone as steely as his eyes. "I can be at your place tomorrow."

"Good. I'll see you bright and early in the morning."

"Morning's full," he informed her. "I'll be there at noon."

Feeling the urge to growl, Hannah turned on her heel and made her way back to her car.

Edginess and anxiety had been Hannah's constant companions ever since her talk with Adam. Was he right? she wondered. Was there something wrong with her independent nature?

No, she kept telling herself. Of course there wasn't.

Tammy and Brian were sitting at the kitchen table, talking. Hannah could see the young man through the front picture window from where she was prepping on the front porch. Now that Hannah knew about

Tammy's beau, her sister felt there was no need to hide her visits with Brian.

As much as she hadn't wanted to like her sister's boyfriend, Hannah had to admit that she'd found Brian to be mannerly, if a little on the shy side. And he treated Tammy with a wondrous gentleness.

Hannah had spent the last half hour sweeping up paint chips off the porch floor and darting covert glances through the window at them. She was amazed by the deep feelings that had evolved in her for Tammy.

She'd come to Little Haven to do what she could for a sister she didn't know, and now she was experiencing some new and complicated emotions that could almost be described as maternal.

Her wristwatch told her she still had an hour to wait for Adam's arrival. She just fumed to think about his free-and-easy attitude toward work. The man seemed to be as ambitious as a slug. How did he ever think to get ahead in life?

The question was like sandpaper against tender skin, and her irritation flared.

She was irritated at Adam for putting off the job of painting the house, and irritated at herself for being attracted to such a...a *lazybones*.

"I've waited long enough," she murmured to the still summer day. She wasn't even sure he'd show up at noon like he'd promised.

That's when she went around back to the shed. She dragged out the rickety old ladder she'd used to scrape the paint from the porch. And then she gathered the paint, the brushes and rollers she'd bought in town. She wouldn't wait for Adam, she'd tackle this job herself.

Instinct told her to start at the top and work down, so she positioned the ladder at one corner and climbed up to paint the porch ceiling. Two dribbles of white pigment ran down her arm, a fat drip plopped on her jaw, before she realized she was filling her brush too full. She swiped at the paint, smearing it across her skin. She'd clean up later.

Every ten minutes or so she'd come down from the ladder and take a quick peek through the window to see that Brian was still seated at the kitchen table. She probably shouldn't worry so much over Tammy and Brian being friends, but she just couldn't shake the nebulous anxiety that gnawed at her.

They're in love, Adam had told Hannah.

Well, something could happen to break them up, Hannah fretted as she climbed the ladder. Tammy could get her heart broken, and Hannah didn't know if her delicate sister could handle such pain and rejection. On the other hand, their relationship might blossom into something deeper, something more... intimate.

The idea had Hannah scrambling down off the ladder. The paintbrush slipped from her fingers. She fumbled to catch it and miscalculated the distance between the two bottom rungs of the ladder. It wobbled precariously, the container of white paint toppling off the ledge. Hannah squealed, reaching out, but in the blink of an eye the can slammed against the porch floor and white paint pooled on the wood. Meaning to snatch up the container to prevent as much mess as possible, she stepped on the edge of the wet brush, lost her balance altogether and ended up sitting directly in the middle of the puddle of thick house paint. Bull's-eye. She couldn't have aimed better if she'd been trying.

Tammy and Brian rushed outside at the sound of all the commotion.

"You okay?" the young man asked.

"I'm fine." Hannah grimaced as paint oozed up into the legs of her shorts.

"I thought Adam was going to do the painting," Tammy said.

"Well, he's not here," Hannah snipped in frustration. "I can't count on him to come when he says he will."

Tammy said, "But it's only noon now."

With infuriating punctuality, Adam chose that moment to drive up the lane. Why of all days, Hannah wondered, did the man have to choose this one to be on time?

Desperate not to get caught sitting in this messy swimming hole of her own making, Hannah hopped to a stand and was immediately rewarded with at least a dozen drips of paint sliding slowly down her legs.

Adam paused at the bottom step of the porch. His eyes gleamed with merriment.

Let him make one teasing comment, Hannah silently vowed, and I will fling this paintbrush right at his chest.

"Tammy, Brian," he greeted, obvious humor suppressed in his tone.

He cleared his throat before addressing her, and Hannah knew he was taking time to rein in his laughter.

"Looks like you started the job without me."

"Yes." She bit off the word like it was a tiny hunk of tough meat, daring him to remark about her predicament.

He gazed up at her work. "Looks nice," he said.

His compliment appeased her, but only a little.

"You'll have to excuse me for just a minute," she told him. "As soon as I get back, we can finish up the ceiling."

With paint seeping into her canvas sneakers, Hannah rushed down the porch steps past Adam and around to the back of the house where she knew she could get her hands on the garden hose.

Apparently, her white-lacquered derriere was more than he could tolerate, for she'd barely rounded the corner of the house when Adam's laughter burst out into the hot summer air.

The house was coming along nicely, Hannah thought. Of course Adam had insisted on taking off Saturday and Sunday to fish with Tammy, to visit with friends, contemplate the clouds, whatever it was he did on the weekends. R & R, he called it. Everyone needs to reflect and rejuvenate, he'd told her.

Hannah saw it as a big waste of time, and that opinion was what had kept her painting when Adam and Tammy and Brian had headed toward the pond with their fishing poles.

However, Adam had returned at noon on Monday. By Wednesday they had nearly completed painting the exterior of the house. And over the course of the job, Hannah had learned a few things about Adam.

He was a hard worker, once he got going, although

he still refused to show up before noon, and she hadn't a clue what he did with his mornings. Her curiosity urged her to question him, but she wouldn't let herself show that kind of interest. It was really none of her business, she realized.

And his judgment of Tammy and Brian's relationship had been correct. The more Hannah saw the two of them together, the more she understood what Adam meant about their affection being innocent. They seemed to be two people enjoying a harmless friendship.

She discovered Adam's love of Little Haven and the people who lived here. He'd told her about attending college in Philadelphia, and how he'd settled there for a time. However, he'd returned to Little Haven because he was happier here, with people he knew and loved, than he'd been anywhere else. Hannah guessed there was something more behind his move back to this small town, but she didn't push the issue. With each passing day, Hannah felt more and more disturbed by Adam's accusation regarding her independent lifestyle. So far she'd held her tongue, afraid that she might start an argument if she were to try to make him understand her need to be self-reliant. But the painting job was nearly done. She was running out of time to make him see why her independence was so important to her.

Hannah had no idea why it was so important to her that she explain herself to him. It just was. And justifying her beliefs seemed to become more pressing with each passing day.

"Well..." Adam descended the ladder. "That's it for me today."

But there are still several hours of daylight left, she wanted to tell him. There was still time for them to work together—*be* together.

The thought made her eyes widen. Heavens, she was so glad she hadn't uttered the thought aloud. What was the matter with her? The important thing was getting the house painted...not that she was spending time with Adam. The heavy feeling in the pit of her belly told her she wasn't so sure anymore.

He set down the paintbrush he'd been using and reached for a bucket. After filling it with water, he dunked the brush into it several times.

"You know," she said haltingly, "you were right the other day."

His brows rose as he looked at her. The pleasant surprise in his expression made her mouth curl up gently at the corners.

"About my being independent, I mean," she finished.

He nodded, obviously remembering their discussion in the park the previous week.

"It's always been very important to me," she went on, "not to be dependent on...on..."

"On any man?" Adam softly supplied.

"On *anyone*," she corrected.

He spent several moments washing the paint from the brush, but his gaze never wavered from her face. The keen curiosity in his silence prompted her to continue with her explanation.

"Adam, I wasn't quite seven years old when my mother took me away from Little Haven." She propped the wide brush she'd been using against the paint can. "She left because there was nothing here for her. She left a husband who had no ambition to make anything of himself. She *had* to leave. If she'd stayed, she would have had to face a life fraught with poverty. Bobby Ray would have sucked every bit of spirit out of her."

Hannah gazed off at the green treetops, then she looked back at Adam. "She moved to New York. She worked hard and made something of herself."

"You mother became independent."

"Exactly," Hannah said.

He sighed, shaking the excess water from the paintbrush he'd been cleaning. Then he pointed at hers, opened his palm in a silent bid for her to hand the brush to him. She picked it up from where she'd placed it near the can and took it to him.

"You're putting an awful lot of stock in your mother's experience," he commented as he dipped her brush into the bucket of water. "So much so," he continued, "that you've formulated your whole way of thinking around it. Do you think that's wise? Seeing as how you only have one side of the story?"

His questions hinted that her mother's actions might somehow have missed the mark of being good and noble.

"Look," she said, "my mother raised me the best she could. She saw to it that I got an education—"

"Sent you to college, did she?"

"Well, no," Hannah said. "I paid the tuition myself." She'd rather die than admit to him that her mother had actually disapproved of her choice of nursing as a career. "But all my achievements were due to the fact that she pushed me and urged me to succeed."

"In becoming independent." Adam swished the brush through the milky-colored water.

Hannah nodded, then frowned as very early memories of handing over her hard-earned baby-sitting money to help pay the rent flashed through her mind.

Your mother was only teaching you to be responsible, a silent voice reminded her.

"In becoming independent," she repeated after him. After a moment of awkward silence she said, "I only told you because...because I wanted you to understand."

Adam shook the water from the second brush and patted it dry with a rag he'd picked up off the picnic table. "So now I do," he finally said.

Chapter Seven

"Can you come?"

The anxiety that turned Adam's handsome face pale frightened Hannah. He'd pushed his way into the back door after only a cursory knock. It was so early she hadn't even had a chance to dress.

"Sure," she told him automatically, setting aside her coffee cup. "What's wrong?"

"It's Mrs. Blake. She's sick."

Hannah was up and moving across the kitchen floor. "Let me throw on some clothes."

During the ride into town, Hannah learned that Little Haven shared one doctor with two other nearby communities, and the closest hospital was nearly an hour's drive away. She was flabbergasted to discover that there were still places—like the tiny town of Little Haven and the hamlets surrounding it—that didn't have adequate medical facilities.

"If I could only get the clinic up and running." His murmur was edged with an underlying frustration.

"Clinic?" Immediate interest sparked to life inside her, forcing the tiny curious question to tumble off her tongue.

"Yeah," he said absently, his attention focused on the winding road ahead. "I've got the building all picked out. I've even got backing from the county. I just need to find someone willing to run it. Someone qualified."

Those two final words seemed to clear the clouds of chaos fogging his mind and had him cocking his head to look at her.

Oh, no, she thought. *No, thank you. I have a job. A good job. In a big hospital that serves tens of thousands of people each year.*

However, before either of them had had a chance to voice their thoughts, Mrs. Blake's house came into view.

The elderly woman was burning with fever as she napped in her big easy chair in the living room.

"She didn't look sick when I saw her on the porch the other day." Hannah whispered the observation.

"She was just getting over a bout of bronchitis," Adam told her.

Nodding, Hannah reached for the woman's wrist and felt a fluttering pulse.

"Looks like she's having a relapse." She wished she had her stethoscope so she could listen to Mrs. Blake's lungs, judge just how much congestion was there. Then Hannah cast a sharp look at Adam. "Not that I'm diagnosing her or anything. I can't do that."

"I'm just asking you to help her," Adam said.

She looked down at Mrs. Blake's soft, wrinkled skin. "I could cool her down a bit. With a cold, damp cloth."

"I'll go round one up."

"Wait, Adam." She pressed her lips together, then asked, "Do you know where she keeps her medicines? The most prevalent cause of relapses is that people don't take all the antibiotics that their doctors prescribe. Check to see if Mrs. Blake has a prescription bottle with pills in it."

"Sure."

When he returned from the back of the house, Adam brought with him a wet washcloth and a brown-tinted plastic bottle.

"You were right," Adam said. "She didn't take all the pills the doctor ordered for her."

He handed them to Hannah. She hesitated.

"Maybe we should wait for her to see the doctor," she said. "He may want to put her on stronger medicine. Her bronchitis may have developed into pneumonia." Worry creased her brow as she said. "I'm not registered in the state of Delaware, Adam."

His tone held gentle admonishment as he told her, "This isn't New York, Hannah. You don't have to worry about being sued. We're all friends and neighbors here. Doing the best for one another that we can."

Hannah doubted that this small town was actually the Nirvana that Adam was trying to make it out to be; however, his love for this elderly woman was apparent. At last Hannah sent Adam for a glass of water, uncapped the bottle and then gently woke Mrs. Blake.

She stayed with the sick woman that day. Tammy

arrived, and Hannah calmed her sister's fears. She assured Tammy that Mrs. Blake would be fine, but that she needed someone to sit with her awhile, to keep her company until the antibiotic began to kill off the infection in her lungs.

Around dinnertime the doctor called and said he couldn't possibly make it back to Little Haven before morning. He was with a patient who was in labor. From his best calculations, he expected the baby to arrive sometime during the night. He didn't dare leave the mother.

Hannah assured the doctor she could handle Mrs. Blake's illness, and as she hung up the phone she couldn't help but marvel that there were people who still chose to give birth at home, not in a hospital with all its modern-day, life-saving technology.

When she voiced this thought to Tammy, she was told, "Oh, I'm sure Penny would love to go to the hospital. But her husband lost his job. And they don't have insurance."

"But, Tammy," she'd tried to explain, "a hospital can't turn you away because you can't pay."

Her sister had shrugged. "But Penny won't go because she can't pay."

Adam came and brought them a carryout meal for dinner and a tin of soup for Mrs. Blake. However, the elderly woman had no appetite, preferring instead to be tucked into her bed which is exactly what Tammy did.

Hannah assured Adam that rest was what Mrs. Blake needed.

Then he said, "Can you stay awhile longer? The refrigerator in the church kitchen is on the fritz and they're planning a chicken and dumpling dinner. I thought I'd swing by and take a look at it."

He looked pulled, like he wanted to help out at the church but he also wanted to stay here with Mrs. Blake. Hannah found his obvious and overwhelming concern quite...endearing.

"I was thinking of spending the night," she told him. The relief and gratitude on his face made her heart sing, made her feel like she was doing something wonderful rather than simply using her nursing skills to tend to a sick stranger.

"Gee, Hannah," he breathed, raking his fingers through his hair, "that would be great. It would sure take a big worry off my mind knowing you're here with her."

For some reason, knowing that she relieved him of a burden made her feel positively giddy.

"You'll be okay?" he asked.

She nodded. "Tammy will be here with me. She hasn't left Mrs. Blake's side all afternoon. In fact, she was the one who suggested we stay."

A shadow passed his features, but it was gone so quickly she had to wonder if she'd even seen it.

She told him, "You go on to the church. And you don't have to stop back here tonight. You look like you need to go home and get some rest."

His head bobbed up and down. "It has been one hell of a day." He paused at the front door. "I'm sorry we didn't get to work on your house today."

"It's okay," she said. "This was much more important." Before she even had time to think, words were slipping from her lips. "I'm going to call the hospital tomorrow and speak to my boss. I'm going to tell her I need to spend more time here."

He looked as if he didn't know what to say, and Hannah felt the same. Spending more time in Little Haven hadn't crossed her mind before that very instant.

The summer evening was quiet as they stood there by Mrs. Blake's front door, both of them seeming to be waiting for something to happen. Finally Adam's blue-gray eyes softened as he gifted her with a soul-stirring smile, and without saying another word, he slipped out into the night.

Looking down from where he was perched on the ladder, paintbrush in hand, Adam paused and enjoyed the way the sun's rays turned Hannah's hair to burnt copper. The ends of her hair brushed the tops of her pink-tinged shoulders. Since they started working on the house together, he constantly reminded her that she needed sunscreen to protect her milky skin.

This woman was an enigma, he'd discovered. A mystery that kept him guessing. And just when he thought he had her figured out, she'd say or do something that turned his whole world on edge.

Take, for instance, her offer to stay the night with Mrs. Blake. He'd been floored by her generous spirit. And every day since then, Hannah had made the trip into town to visit with the elderly woman.

Of course, he'd been bothered by the fact that Hannah had used Tammy as the excuse behind her offer to stay with Mrs. Blake. But she had stayed, and he guessed that's what had been important.

He hadn't meant to reveal his dream of the clinic

to Hannah. He wasn't quite sure yet she was the sort of person in whom he could place that kind of trust. The clinic was a project he'd been working on for so long, and the frustration and worry he'd been feeling about Mrs. Blake had caused the thought to flow from him before he'd been able to stop it. Once he had told Hannah about the clinic, he'd had the thought that she would be the perfect person to make his dream come true. But as quickly as the idea had entered his mind, he'd dismissed it. Hannah would never consider such a position. Her job up north was simply too important to her. She'd made that clear enough.

The almost audible humming that seemed to connect them whenever they were together must have alerted her that he was staring. She stopped painting and looked up at him.

He smiled. She was the most beautiful woman he'd ever set eyes on. He should feel awkward that she'd caught him watching her. But he didn't.

"Adam?"

"Hmm?" he answered, having every intention of continuing with his work. But for the life of him he couldn't seem to move, couldn't look away. Every ounce of his attention was riveted to her face, the tiny creases that bracketed her luscious mouth, the tiny dimple he knew would appear if he could make her smile wide enough.

"I—I'd like to ask you something."

Her obvious agitation intrigued him, and he came down the ladder. He put down the brush and reached into his back pocket for a rag. Absently he wiped his hands clean.

"It's, um," she haltingly began, "it's about this weekend."

He watched her swipe at the wisps of hair framing her face, the smudge of white paint on her cheekbone somehow making her features cuter than ever.

"Tammy's been bugging me about it," she continued. "Apparently there's some sort of dance at the community center. And she wants to go. I mean, she's asked Brian and they plan to go. I think it would be good if I went. To keep an eye on the two of them. What do you think?"

Adam suppressed a grin. He knew about the Sadie Hawkins dance taking place this Saturday night. It was an evening where the women took the initiative to ask out their favorite beau. However, he never would have guessed that Hannah might ask him to take her.

He was disappointed that once again she seemed to be using her sister as an excuse behind her actions. Adam didn't plan to make this easy for her.

"I think you should go," he told her. "Not that Brian and Tammy need a baby-sitter. What I think you need is to have a good time."

Embarrassment tinted her cheeks pinker than the sun already had. It was adorable, he thought.

"W-well," she stammered, "what I was thinking…was that maybe you'd…maybe—" She took a moment to swallow. "If you're not busy, do you think you might go with me?" Without waiting for him to answer, she rushed headlong into her next litany. "I know you're awfully busy. And it's not something you'd normally do. Me, neither. But…it might be fun. It might be—"

Why did she have such a difficult time admitting the attraction vibrating between them? he wondered. What had happened in her life that made it so hard for her to concede to what she was feeling?

"You know," Hannah told him, "Tammy's not going to leave me alone until I've finally told her that I asked you."

The kiss they had shared had rocked him to the very soles of his feet. The wild passion she'd unleashed on him had been steamy hot. The memory of it had burned through his achy, erotic dreams. Night visions filled with her sweet lips, her jewel-green eyes.

Every instinct in him had told him to stay miles away from Hannah, but he hadn't been able to do that. And he knew why. He wanted her. Just like she so obviously wanted him. Hell, she'd *told* him she wanted him. But that confession had been followed by her declaring that she couldn't allow herself to become involved with him, that her life up north took precedence.

Maybe she was changing her mind.

But if so, why was she still using Tammy as an excuse?

Hannah licked her lips, her tongue sliding sensuously across her dusky skin. "If you don't want to go, I'll understand."

He studied her a moment, feeling as though she was as complicated as an intricate maze. If a man were to chance getting lost in her, he just might solve the puzzle...and find a wonderful reward for his trouble.

Or, a silent voice warned, *he just might lose himself altogether.*

"I'll go."

Hannah suddenly felt like a high-school-aged teeny-bopper. She stood in front of the mirror surveying her image.

Why had she gotten all caught up in Tammy's excitement? she wondered. Why had she agreed to borrow this skimpy little sundress from her sister? Yes, Tammy had been so happy this afternoon when they had spent time choosing what they would wear to the dance. And Hannah had almost become teary-eyed when Tammy had hugged her tight and said that there was nothing better than having a sister to share things with.

But did this dress have to show so much…skin? She tugged the spaghetti strap back up onto her shoulder.

The revealing outfit might not be her usual style, Hannah noted, but she couldn't help but feel that the last two weeks of working out in the sun had done marvelous things to her. Her skin glowed golden from the sun, and she didn't think it was just her imagination when she thought that her muscles were more taut, more firm. She looked good, even if she did say so herself.

Running a brush through her hair, she wondered if Adam would think so, too.

That doesn't matter, she chastised herself. You're going to this shindig tonight so you can keep an eye on Tammy and Brian…*not* to turn Adam's head.

Still, she thought, it wouldn't be half-bad if he were to notice her just a little, would it?

Grinning ruefully, she tossed the brush on the bureau. *Oh, he notices you, all right. That's something you've known from the very beginning. Ignoring the attention he's been giving you has been your biggest problem—*

"Oh, hush already," she whispered to the empty room.

Would it be so bad if she were to follow her sister's advice and have a little fun for once in her life? Hannah reached out and tugged her purse off the bedroom doorknob. What she planned to do was ignore that scolding voice in her head and enjoy the evening.

"We're going to be late!" Tammy called from downstairs.

Hannah hurried down the stairs. "Then I guess we'd better get a move on."

The sisters left the house, arm in arm, laughing, and Hannah didn't think she'd ever felt so carefree.

The community center's main hall had been decorated with hundreds of brightly colored balloons. Streamers looped from rafter to rafter high overhead. Fake ficus trees flanked the walls, each one sprinkled with glittering white lights. The effect was gorgeous and extremely romantic.

A man stood on the stage nearly hidden behind huge speakers. He couldn't really be called a disc jockey as he uttered not one word, but only changed the records, one after another. However, the crowd didn't seem to mind as long as he kept the music playing.

Hannah's mouth curled up at the corners when Tammy asked Brian for yet another dance, but her smile faded as she turned and found Adam staring at her.

Just looking at him made her heart leap in her chest like a gazelle. He was so handsome in his smoke-gray sport coat and casual trousers. She was relieved that she'd worn Tammy's sundress and not the more formal blue silk outfit she'd brought with her to Little Haven.

She wished he'd say something. But so far he'd been happy to watch the dancers or pass a quick greeting to the people he knew, which seemed like just about everyone in the room. Hannah sat quietly, content for the moment to simply study his profile.

His bronzed skin glowed with health. When he smiled, his eyes crinkled at the corners, and the tiny creases at the edges of his mouth were evidence that he laughed often.

Her work at the hospital put her in contact with men every single day: doctors, administrators, patients. Some of them were exceptionally handsome. So why had she not been affected by them the way she was by Adam? Why had she not experienced these heart-pounding, pulse-racing reactions before now?

He turned and looked at her, the clear, bright whites of his eyes making the gray-blue of his irises stand out strikingly. Awkwardness wove its way around them, like a spindly spider constructing its web.

"Did I tell you that sunflowers become you?"

His voice was so low, so achingly sensuous, that

Hannah's breath caught in her throat. For a moment she didn't think she'd be able to speak. She glanced down at the dress she wore, at the large, yellow-petaled flowers decorating the fabric.

"I-it's Tammy's."

"You look lovely."

The constraint between them seemed to swell and strain. She tried to smile, but failed miserably. This man made her feel like such a schoolgirl. All giddy and clumsy with overwhelming emotion.

"Thanks."

"So," he said, his tone dropping to a mere whisper, "how long do I have to wait?"

A frown of confusion buckled her brow.

"Wait?" Then he glanced out at the men and women dancing, and she realized to what he was referring.

"I—I wanted to ask you to dance, but..." She bit her lip. She hated feeling so awkward. So innocent. So unworldly. "But I was feeling a little embarrassed."

His tenderhearted smile sent a delighted shiver coursing across every inch of her skin.

"Well, the ice is broken now," he told her. "Think you can manage a proposal?"

A proposal? Her eyes widened.

To dance, a silent voice taunted her.

She nodded to cover her chagrin. After moistening her lips and garnering her courage, she said, "Can we..." She faltered. "How about..." She frowned and then tried yet again. "Is it okay...Would you like it if..."

Finally he chuckled outright, took her hand and

pulled her to her feet. "Come on," he said. "If we wait for you to get the invitation out, we'll be as old as the hills before we get out on the dance floor."

His laughter was infectious, and she allowed herself to be led out among the other dancers.

The beat of the melody was swift, and Adam's moves were smooth and graceful. He obviously enjoyed the music, even silently mouthed the words. Luckily it was a song Hannah knew, too. Before long they were singing it together between chortles and snickers whenever one or the other of them made a mistake.

The strains faded away, and a new song began to play. A slow, sexy tune. And the couples on the dance floor began to cozy up.

Adam placed the flat of one hand on the small of her back and took her hand with the other. He smelled so good, earthy and mysterious and male, and Hannah closed her eyes and drank in the aroma of him. The room was hot, and his body heat only added to her rising temperature.

"I've got an idea," he whispered, the tug of his hand in hers urging her to follow him. Despite her disappointment of having their slow dance interrupted, Hannah allowed herself to be led.

He pushed open the side door, and she sighed as a light breeze brushed across her skin.

"Better?" he asked.

"Much."

She'd expected that their dance was over, that Adam meant for them to simply stand outside and cool themselves. However, the music played on, albeit faint and much more subtle out here in the dark, and he obviously intended to take advantage of the seclusion.

Here alone with him, she felt electrified. Like she'd been dormant, asleep, and someone had flipped a switch that started a heated current circulating throughout her body. She'd been aware of Adam from the very first—she couldn't deny it even though she wanted to with all her might, even though she tried to—but that cognizance was now totally overwhelming. Like an ultrahigh voltage surging through her. Stirring every muscle and sinew in her. Shocking her into action.

She wanted this man. Badly. And she decided at that very instant that at some time during this fabulous night she'd let him know exactly how she felt.

Chapter Eight

Wine was a great courage amplifier, and Hannah used it liberally. She laughed and flirted and danced with her handsome date. And Adam laughed and flirted and danced with her. She wished the night would never end. But eventually it did.

When Adam plucked the keys from her fingers and gently suggested he would drive, she didn't argue. He dropped off Brian and then drove Hannah and Tammy home.

"'Night, Adam," Tammy said, and she ran up the porch steps and into the house.

Hannah found the summer heat just as intoxicating as the alcohol pumping through her bloodstream.

"You don't have to go just yet, do you?" Almost of their own accord, her lips pouted prettily and she nearly giggled.

"No." His voice was as soft as the velvet night and extremely sedate. "I don't have to go."

"Ooh, goody!" This time she did giggle.

The sound she heard emitting from her throat didn't sound childish or in any way immature. It sounded free. It *felt* free. And the giddiness jumping around inside her offered her an awesome liberty—liberty to say, to *do*, anything she pleased. And it was exhilarating.

"Let's sit on the porch." Intending to bound up the steps, she tripped when her toe caught on the very first rise.

"Whoa there," Adam said, catching her in his arms.

All the wine she'd consumed was doing strange things to her hand-eye coordination but it was a relief to know that the alcohol did nothing to her mental state. Her judgment was well intact.

She nestled against his chest, gazed up into his face. "You saved me," she whispered. "You're my hero."

Humor rumbled deep in his throat, and she felt the vibration of it, sexy and strong, against her jaw and palm.

"Come on," he told her. "Let's go sit down before you fall down."

She sensed he was laughing at her, and she couldn't fathom why he'd do such a thing. But she really didn't care. She felt so good, so...unconstrained.

They slowly made their way up the porch stairs and then settled themselves on the wooden swing. The rusty springs complained just a bit as they sat down, and their weight set the bench swing into motion.

"It's so peaceful here, Adam," she murmured,

snuggling against him. He smelled so good. Felt so good. She couldn't seem to get close enough.

"*Peaceful* is a perfect word to describe Little Haven."

Adam let her curl up against him, even placing a protective arm around her shoulders. His heart thumped, steady and strong, under her splayed hand, the heat of him seeping through the front of his dress shirt. Her thoughts were deliciously fuzzy, and she offered him a coy smile. His sexy mouth curled languidly in response, and a deep and heady craving welled up in her.

"Kiss me." And she tugged lightly on his shirtfront, conveying urgency in her demand.

His lips were hot and insistent against hers. Or wait, she wondered hazily, was it *her* mouth that was hot and insistent against his? The quandary confused her momentarily, but she released the shadowy thought, and it floated away like a helium balloon, up, up, up into the starry sky. And she let the rest of her thoughts drift away as well. Right now she didn't want to think. Right now she only wanted to feel.

She pressed ardent kisses against his lips, his jaw, his neck. She was vaguely aware that his breathing had become ragged, the rough sound of it stoking the fire of her passion. Again she felt she couldn't seem to get close enough to him. Grasping his shoulders, she lifted herself, sliding onto his lap.

His hands seemed to be everywhere at once, on her bare forearms, gliding up her back, settling on her waist, skimming up to cup and then gently knead her breasts. The thin cotton fabric of the sundress was very little protection against his touch. However, protection was the last thing she wanted.

Every instinct in her shouted and screamed for her to reach around and unzip her dress, to slide the thin straps over her shoulders and give him full, unencumbered access to her body. She wanted to experience the feel of his hands on her bare flesh, the parts of her that had never before been touched by a man.

The soft, sibilant sound of Hannah's zipper being unfastened broke, clear and crystalline, through the clouds of Adam's heart-racing passion. Without thinking, he reached around and placed a quelling hand on her fingers.

"Wait." The word he uttered sounded craggy and uneven like a piece of roughly torn paper.

He wanted to touch her, to see the moonlight spilling over her beautiful body, to taste her hot, voluptuous skin. Oh, how he wanted those things.

But he had to stop her. She wasn't thinking clearly. She'd had too much to drink. He knew that. And he couldn't take advantage of it. No matter how badly he might want to.

"What? Don't you want to...?"

Her questions held evident confusion, and he wondered how he could explain his actions without offending her.

"Let's just slow down for a minute," he told her. "I need a little time."

"Too racy for you, am I?"

Her sensuously teasing chuckle was nearly his undoing, and for an instant he considered unzipping her dress and tugging it off her himself. But then her fingers released the plastic fastener, her hands lowering to her sides, and she rested her head against his shoulder.

Oh, yes, he wanted to croon to her, *you're much too racy for me.* This woman had gotten to him, again and again, since her arrival into town. She'd made him experience wild dips in his emotions. Extremely high highs, exceedingly low lows, and fears and doubts that were enough to fell even the strongest and bravest of men. He wondered if she realized these things.

"Tonight," she whispered against his chest, "I almost felt like I'd finally attended my first school dance."

The unwitting grunt he emitted must have conveyed his surprise. First school dance? As in *high school?*

"Oh, there were plenty of opportunities," she continued. "There was the sophomore semiformal, the junior and senior proms, lots of student get-togethers. But I was too busy working to accept any invitations to any of them."

A teenager having a part-time job during high school wasn't such a bad thing, Adam mused. He'd worked in the local garage himself when he'd been a teen. Made enough money to cover his car insurance and gasoline costs. The two most important things to a high school male.

However, Hannah's claim that she was too busy to attend any school dances didn't make any sense. Employers and parents alike understood the need for adolescents to be social. He remained quiet, silently hoping she'd elaborate.

"I got my first baby-sitting job when I was ten," she said, sighing softly, her body settling in against his. "I kept those kids until their mom got home from work all through middle school. My mother wanted me to start saving for college early. She knew my dad wouldn't help out with the cost of educating me, so she told me I'd have to pay for it on my own. She said it would be a good lesson in responsibility." Again she sighed. "I guess it was. Although I missed not being part of my school's volleyball team."

She started baby-sitting at ten? But at ten years old she was just a youngster herself. He placed his hands on her hips to stop her squirming. The constant movement of her softly rounded bottom against his lap was agony.

"As soon as I started high school, my mother decided it was time for me to start buying my own clothes and paying a share of the rent." Her voice grew sleepy. "So I lied about my age and got a full-time job."

A freshman...that would have made her about fifteen. Working forty hours a week? That was illegal, wasn't it? There were child labor laws to prevent that sort of practice. Legal or not, it sounded as though Hannah had had her mother's blessing.

"So I saved for college and paid my bills," Hannah said. "As soon as I could get out on my own, I did. I was independent. I've always been independent. I'm sure my mother's very proud."

Her breath on his ear had him turning toward her. He knew her eyes were green, but the velvety night made it impossible for him to make out their color. The dark orbs searched his face.

There was sadness in her voice, in her gaze. A sadness he didn't believe she was even aware of.

Hannah's mother hadn't been much of a parent, in Adam's estimation. She'd abandoned her youngest daughter altogether and then shoved her oldest out on her own much too early. Bobby Ray might not have been able to provide monetarily for Tammy, but Adam couldn't help but feel that the youngest Cavanaugh sister had been blessed with the better deal.

"My, you smell good," Hannah breathed. Then she said, "I'm tired."

He reached up and slid his fingers down the length of her silken jaw. "I can imagine. You need to go inside and get some sleep."

She smiled, and Adam felt his heart kick like a mule.

"I'm not *that* tired," she said. "Come inside. Go to bed with me."

His need for her had cooled. Oh, he still wanted her. Terribly. Desire still throbbed like a toothache low in his belly. But all the while she'd talked, he'd had the chance to rein in his passion. So he barely hesitated before saying, "Not tonight, my Hannah. Not tonight."

When they finally did make love—and there was no doubt in his mind that they would—he wanted her clearheaded, with no shadowy recollections of her childhood darkening the experience, no alcohol in her blood blurring the fiery memory of their time together. No, he wanted her mind filled with one thought alone.

Him!

* * *

Hannah couldn't believe she was traipsing through the woods so early on a Sunday morning. She'd awakened feeling amazingly fresh, wonderfully warm. Her memories of last night were a bit on the foggy side, but she did remember one thing: Adam had not taken advantage of her.

She vaguely recalled having come on to him. Even now her face flamed at what was sure to have been her shameless behavior. But she'd been determined to show him how she was feeling, and if memory served, she'd done just that.

However, Adam had been as chivalrous as a knight in shining armor. *Her* knight in shining armor.

And she realized just as soon as she'd opened her eyes this morning that he'd turned down her offer because he understood that she'd had too much to drink. He simply was too good, too purehearted to use her in any way that might seem injurious to her or selfish on his part.

Her whole body hummed with happiness, her heart sang in harmony with the birds in the trees. Is this what love felt like?

Hannah stopped. The startling question turned her knees so weak that she was forced to press her palms against the rough bark of a tree for momentary support.

Love? Did she love Adam?

The idea was just too daunting for her to ponder right now. She simply wasn't prepared...wasn't ready to examine her feelings that closely.

The house came into view. Tammy had told her he didn't live far from them. Luckily his truck was parked in front so she knew she had caught him before he'd left for the local fishing hole or whatever it was he spent his mornings doing. Hannah broke into a jog.

She didn't know if she was running toward Adam and the wonderful way he made her heart sing, or fleeing the intimidating concept of love. The notion was confusing. Too confusing. She shoved the thoughts right out of her head, and after crossing the pea stone drive, she took the porch steps two at a time.

Several moments passed before he finally opened the door.

"Hannah." Surprise was evident in his tone. "What's wrong?"

"Does something have to be wrong for me to come to see you?" She sidled past him, trying hard not to sound breathless and excited, trying hard not to stare at his broad, bare chest and lean, jeans-clad hips. Instead she put a great deal of effort into surveying his lovely log cabin. Finally she commented, "You've got a great place."

He murmured his thanks as he shut the door. "It's small, but it's home."

The living room, kitchen and eating area were all one big open space. The wall of windows let in lots of light. At the end of the small hallway, an open door revealed a corner of his rumpled bed, the blanket and sheet cascading onto the floor. She grinned. That was the very place she intended to be—*with Adam*— if her visit played out as she hoped.

Spinning around, she offered him a bright smile. And then nearly chuckled as she took in his disheveled hair, his bare feet.

"Looks like I woke you," she said.

He shook his head. "Nope. A man's gotta be asleep before he can be awakened." He moved into the kitchen area. "How about some coffee?"

She'd never wanted to be seductive before...prior to last night, of course, when the wine she'd practically guzzled had provided such a boost to her self-confidence. How would a temptress accept an invitation for coffee? she wondered. When nothing came to her, she simply answered, "Sure."

Rekindling some of last night's sauciness was what she needed. A blurry memory came to her. Had she really been bold enough to ask him to come to bed with her? She should be embarrassed over her behavior. But all she could feel was this heart-wrenching gratitude that he hadn't taken advantage of the situation. He very well could have. But instead, when her defenses had been down, when her judgment had been impaired, he had seen to it that she was taken care of. For some reason that made Adam all the more appealing to her.

The thought urged her to say, "I came to thank you."

He remained silent as he stood at the sink filling the coffeepot with water, but she could see curiosity lighting his blue-gray eyes when he looked at her.

"I was a little...drunk last night," she began to explain. "And I want you to know I appreciate how you—" She felt her cheeks flush with heat. Her voice grew shaky as she finished, "Took care of me."

Something about those four little words made her pause. For some reason she felt that what she'd just said should have overwhelmed her...should have had some kind of earth-shattering effect on her; however, she was too involved in wooing Adam to pay too much attention to the notion.

"You could have...*had* me last night." The past-tense verb tumbled breathlessly from her lips, describing, revealing—she hoped—so much of how she was feeling, what she was thinking.

"Maybe," he muttered. "But I want a woman to be clearheaded, to know exactly what it is she's doing."

A few steps and she was next to him, her hip leaning provocatively against the kitchen counter, only a fraction of an inch from where his strong, tanned fingers curled over the edge. Her chin lowered as she leveled a most tantalizing gaze on him. "Well, I'm stone-cold sober this morning."

The coffeepot came to rest on the countertop, forgotten, as he stared back at her, searching her eyes.

Good, she thought. She had his attention. But then, after that bold, unmistakable invitation, how could she not?

"I came over this morning—" the top button of her blouse came unfastened with the tiniest movement of her fingers "—to show you just how much I appreciate your gallant behavior last night."

His blue gaze darkened with sudden and obvious desire, lowering and then riveting to the vee opening of her blouse, and with an excruciating slowness she undid the second button to reveal more skin, a bit more cleavage.

The air in the wide-open room seemed to grow thick and hot, and the excited anticipation that made her pulse pound also had her feeling short-winded.

The utter quiet was disturbed only by the slow but ever-growing sense of expectation.

Adam's eyes darted up to her face, his jaw tensing to what looked to be the point of pain. "Look," he said, then he grew still. He moistened his lips, inhaled slow and deep, like he was mulling over something, making some decision or other. Finally he continued, "I don't deserve any thanks. Any decent human being could have seen that you were a little...tipsy."

Spontaneous laughter bubbled from her throat. "I was drunk as a skunk," she quipped with an impish grin.

His brow creased, and he turned from her, reaching up to snatch a paper filter from the shelf and stuff it into the basket of the coffee maker. Then, popping off the lid to the can of coffee, he began spooning in the preground beans.

He gave her a darting glance. "Hannah," he began, then his tone faded away into nothing as he seemingly focused all his attention on filling the coffee machine's water chamber.

Vaguely aware of the fact that he didn't chuckle at her self-deprecating remark, she grew a little uneasy. Something was wrong. Something had happened between last night and this morning. He'd wanted her last night. She'd have bet her soul on it. So why...

He flipped the switch that started the coffee brewing and then directed his gaze on her. "I don't want you to be offended by what I'm about to say," he told her.

His tone was quiet, controlled and utterly deliberate. She clamped her bottom lip between her teeth. She'd heard those words, or something akin to them, many times. From her mother. And each and every time, what followed was *always* something that wounded.

"I'm not interested in casual sex."

Until now, her fingers had been toying absently with the facing of her blouse, but the sound of his flat, emphatic statement caused them to grow still. His rejection was like a razor to her heart, slashing and ripping at the most vulnerable part of her. Her mouth went dry, her whole body heating from the embarrassment of the situation.

She'd offered herself to him, and he'd turned her down. Flat.

Last night he'd returned her kisses, touched her in a way that told her he wanted her. So why this slap in the face? she wondered.

"I r-really—" her voice sounded hollow and distant "—should go." She took a backward step.

"Wait a minute," he said. Evidently realizing her distress, he reached out to her.

She slapped his hands away. Shaking her head frantically, she stressed, "It's okay. It's really okay." And then she felt a tremendous need to force some kind of normalcy into this abnormal moment. "I'm sorry I can't stay for coffee." She wrenched the lie from down deep in her gut as breezily as she could manage, but it missed the mark by a long shot.

"Don't leave like this."

"It's okay," she repeated. She tugged open the door and bolted.

She raced through the woods, oblivious to the birds singing in the trees, blind to her sun-dappled surroundings.

Even though turmoil reigned supreme in her head, a still, silent voice told her she could overcome this humiliation, she could live with the embarrassment. Everything was going to be okay.

Tears welled in her eyes, blurring her vision and turning the sunlit path before her into the rainbow hues seen through a glass prism.

She would not cry over that man. She was a strong, independent woman. Dashing away the tears, she once again told herself that everything was okay. That *she* was okay. She'd told Adam as much. Now she only had to make herself believe it.

She was okay. She *was!*

But for the first time in her life she realized that she wasn't.

Chapter Nine

"So did you and Adam do it?"

Hannah was too preoccupied wallowing in her misery to pay much attention to her sister's question. "Do what?" she asked, tugging, pulling and finally yanking out yet another weed growing in the infested flower beds.

Her entire morning had been spent tackling this jungle they called a lawn. The grass had been so high in some spots that the ancient mower kept getting clogged and even cut off several times. It had been frustrating, backbreaking work, but it had been just what she needed.

The time she'd spent in the hot sun was, in her estimation, just the punishment she deserved for letting down her guard against Adam. Time and again her mother had lectured her about men and how the opposite sex did nothing but drag a woman down.

And there she went, traipsing over there with every intention of—

"You know..."

Tammy once more disrupted her train of thought.

"*It.* I figured that's why you went to see Adam this morning."

The hushed, scandalous tone of her sister's voice made Hannah blink. She straightened her spine, absently swiping the back of her grimy hand across her damp brow as she leveled her gaze on Tammy.

Adam was forgotten for the moment as her frenzied thoughts went into a panic over what Tammy could mean. Surely she wasn't referring to...

"*It?*" Hannah asked. "What do you mean, *it?*"

"Oh, you know." Her sister's face tinged pink. "*It.*"

Heavens above! Tammy *was* talking about...well, about *it.*

Hannah's eyes widened; her heart fluttered. She'd never had cause to discuss intimacy before. With anyone. And especially not with a young woman with a diminished mental capacity. She felt the need to tread very carefully.

"Honey," Hannah began, "what do you know about..." Her question faded into silence when she couldn't decide on the right word to use.

"*It?*" Tammy laughed. "A long time ago, Daddy told me a little about the birds and the bees. I think he wanted to make sure nobody hurt me. And Adam told me some, too."

What! a voice in her head wanted to scream. *What did he tell you?*

"Once Brian and I became friends," Tammy explained, almost as if she'd heard Hannah's silent, frantic question, "Adam told me where babies come from." She cocked her head, squinting in the bright sunlight. "So, did you?"

"Did we?" she murmured, having forgotten the original question. The subject came back to her like a swift kick in the rear. "Oh." Nibbling her lip, she took a moment to ponder her answer.

Avoidance, she decided, was her best bet.

"Honey, what makes you think that's why I went over to see Adam this morning?"

One side of Tammy's delicate mouth quirked up jauntily. "When you left the house you had that look in your eyes."

That look? Hannah wondered. What had her sister seen in her expression this morning?

"You were just like one of those women on TV," Tammy continued. "You know. Those women on the soap operas. Those hungry women."

Hannah's voice was a mere whisper when she parroted, "Hungry?"

There was no trace of lewdness in Tammy's voice, only an innocent matter-of-factness when she elaborated, "Hungry for a man."

Hannah's fingers flew to her mouth and she gasped. Bits of dirt and grass clung to her lips, and she coughed and sputtered. Heavens above! One would think *she* was the naive one here.

Adam had told her that Tammy and Brian's relationship was innocent, and from that Hannah had simply assumed that her sister was too guileless to even know anything about intimacy between a man and a woman. However, here Tammy was talking about the subject in a manner that was very straightforward—with the emphasis on *forward.* Too forward. Too personal.

That would be her saving grace, Hannah decided, almost giddy with relief when she realized she wouldn't have to expose her humiliating experience at Adam's earlier.

"Tammy," she said, "don't you think this conversation is a bit...personal? I mean, there are plenty of things we can talk about. We don't need to discuss—"

The sentence came to an abrupt end as Hannah once again tried to find just the right words to describe what it was they were talking about. Her nurse's training kicked in, and terms began floating in her head: intercourse, sex, copulation. But none of them seemed soft enough, gentle enough to use in a conversation with a young woman as unknowing as Hannah had thought, had *hoped,* her sister was.

"Gee, Hannah," Tammy said, disappointment evident in her tone, "we're sisters. We should be able to talk about anything. About everything."

Guilt rolled over Hannah like a heavy cloud.

"I would tell you," her sister continued, "if Brian and I did it."

No! Hannah's subconscious shouted. *That's something I'm better off not knowing.*

She quickly remembered that taking care of Tammy had been her one and only reason for coming to this little town. And how could she do that if she shied away from important conversations like this one?

Then she comprehended what it was—exactly—

that Tammy had said. She *would* tell, as in describing something that was to happen in the future, which meant that she and Brian *hadn't*.

The realization caused her shoulders to sag with relief. Then the professional nurse in Hannah took over again as she thought of all the things she wanted to tell Tammy, starting off with the responsibility of using birth control. Because, like it or not, Hannah was talking to an adult. A grown woman fully capable of experiencing sexual urges. A grown woman fully capable of surrendering to those urges.

"You're right, honey." Hannah unwittingly rubbed her smudgy palms together. "We should be able to talk about anything and everything."

Tammy's green eyes glittered with anticipation. "So, did you and Adam do it?"

Just keep this simple and honest, she told herself. *And please, please,* a silent voice begged, *don't let Tammy ask for details.* Hannah didn't think she'd survive if she had to recount those mortifying moments she'd spent with Adam this morning. Describing her humiliation was the last thing she was prepared for right now.

"No," she finally answered, "we didn't."

Tossing her head back, Tammy let out a gurgle of laughter that startled Hannah.

"I didn't think he'd do it," she said, a satisfied grin playing around the corners of her mouth.

Immediately Hannah felt her muscles constrict with an unpleasant indignation. Why would Tammy think such a thing? What could he have said to her that would make her surmise that he wasn't willing to be intimate with Hannah? Then, unwittingly, she began to wonder what might be wrong with her that Adam would reject her. Maybe he didn't like strawberry-blondes. Maybe her hips were a little too wide for his taste.

Showing interest in what Adam thought of her was the last thing she should be doing, she thought. She shouldn't give a hoot what he thought or how he felt. However, even if there was some reason he found her unattractive, he had no right discussing his feelings with Tammy. And no matter how hard she tried to tamp down her curiosity regarding what he told her sister, the overwhelming need to know completely swamped her.

As nonchalantly as possible Hannah asked, "What makes you say that? Did Adam say something to you that makes you think he finds me unattractive?"

"Oh, no," Tammy admitted. "He never said a word about you. But he did tell me and Brian that he believes in love. In marriage. And most important, he said he believes in lifetime commitment."

Her sister went on to explain how Adam stressed the need for two people to really know each other before they got caught up in the physical side of love, before they "do it" as Tammy phrased it. Hannah realized that this sexual discussion, of sorts, that Adam had had with Tammy was his way of protecting her, his way of protecting her and Brian from doing something they simply weren't ready for.

This information also revealed more about Adam. And, once again, Hannah was forced to respect him. He hadn't been afraid to take the responsibility of enlightening Tammy and Brian about human nature. Hannah's chest grew tight, her heart warmed. A knot formed in her throat and her eyes welled with emotion. Adam was truly an extraordinary man. She thought about all he had done for Tammy, and she realized he was a man who felt a deep obligation toward those around him. He was also a man for whom she had come to care deeply. More deeply than she wanted to admit.

When the daunting idea of love had come into her head this morning on her way to his house, she'd shoved it away, too fearful to examine it. But now she had no other choice but to finally admit the truth: she loved Adam. Fiercely.

That realization should have made her heart soar. But instead Hannah felt bleak inside. It was just her luck to discover how she felt about the man right on the heels of having to swallow the bitter pill of his rejection.

"If Adam wanted me and Brian to wait," Tammy commented, "until we could say that we were committed to each other for all our lives, then I'm sure that's what he wants for himself, too."

Tammy had put all the pieces of the puzzle together, Hannah mused, smiling. Her mentally challenged baby sister really was smarter than she'd given her credit for.

But her smile quickly faded as she was hit with another huge realization.

Adam hadn't really rejected her completely. He'd simply said he wasn't interested in *casual* sex.

He *was* attracted to her. Those vibes she'd been feeling between them since coming to town just couldn't be denied. And when they had kissed, Adam's response had been hot, needy.

Adrenaline surged through her. All at once, it became so clear. Adam hadn't rejected her because he wasn't interested...he'd turned down her sensual offer because he wanted more than just sex.

He was looking for a lifetime commitment. Like Tammy had told her, he believed in marriage.

Her emotions took another nosedive as, once again, Hannah understood that her mother's lectures were ringing true. *Men always wanted more than a woman was able to offer. And a man would take and take and take until he sucked a woman dry.*

A commitment to Adam would mean giving up too much. She was on a path. Her *chosen* path. She had goals just within her reach. Goals she'd worked hard at her whole life. Was it fair for her to have to abandon her path, her goals, for the love of a man?

Adam didn't visit Tammy, didn't even call to check on her, the rest of the weekend. And by Monday afternoon plenty of time had passed for Hannah's bitterness to build to a frightening peak. Who did he think he was to want her to alter her life for him?

Of course, he hadn't said that's what he wanted. But, like Tammy, Hannah was able to gather all the little pieces of the puzzle and put them together.

He'd said several times that taking Tammy to New York was the wrong thing. That Hannah ought to stay in Little Haven for her sister's sake. And his unspoken, yet nonetheless apparent, suggestion that Hannah was the person to organize and run his proposed health clinic had been yet another ploy to get her to move here.

Granted, those were all reasons based on his belief

in what was best for Tammy. However, the situation had grown much more personal when she'd offered herself to him and he'd turned her down.

Even though she now highly suspected that *dis*interest hadn't been his motivation—to the contrary, actually—the memory of last Saturday morning still made her burn with mortification.

Since she hadn't seen or heard from him since the incident, Hannah had come to the conclusion that he wouldn't show up again to help her finish painting the house. So she was surprised when he arrived promptly at noon on Monday.

"Afternoon," he called to her in solemn greeting.

She gave him an unsmiling nod in response, but her heart felt like it was going to pound a hole right through her chest.

Damn it! She would not allow herself to react to him. She would not!

He rounded the corner of the house without another word. Hannah followed him a few minutes later and saw that he'd wasted no time in getting to work. The glistening wooden paddle balancing on the rim of the metal can lid was evidence that he'd opened and stirred the paint. He had already climbed the ladder leaning against the side of the house, a bucket of paint hanging from his grip.

Good, Hannah thought. *We should finish this job today and I won't have to suffer being near him.*

She snatched up what she'd come to call her favorite stiff-bristled brush, grabbed a bucket of paint for herself and set to work.

They worked for more than an hour without speaking. He climbed down off the ladder twice to reposition it.

Working in silence was nothing new for them, Hannah thought. It was the *kind* of silence that was different. Before his rejection of her, the silences between them had sometimes been easy, like a quiet camaraderie. But most often the silences had been tense with that humming awareness. She discovered that either of those were preferable to these hushed moments. The air felt stiff. Heavy. Terribly awkward. And it rubbed against Hannah's nerves until they felt raw and frayed.

His rejection had devastated her, yesterday morning. She had thought she'd realized her deep feelings for Adam only to have him cast them aside like they—and she—were meaningless to him. However, after talking with Tammy, Hannah surmised that Adam had refused her offer *because she wasn't offering enough.*

Maybe she was completely wrong. Maybe the pieces she'd put together didn't fit at all into the picture she'd formed in her head.

But did it really matter either way? she wondered.

If Adam had rejected her because he wasn't interested, then, fine. There wasn't much she could do about that. And if he'd declined to sleep with her because she wasn't offering him everything—the world, her life on a silver platter—then there wasn't much she could do about that, either. A woman could only offer so much.

A man will take and take and take until he sucks a woman dry.

The idea stirred the embers of her anger.

Hannah wouldn't let Adam...or any other man for that matter...suck her bone-dry of everything that made her who she was: her hopes, her dreams, her goals.

When Adam descended the ladder for the third time, Hannah was sure he'd move it over to the corner of the house, the last section that needed painting. But he didn't. Instead he set down his bucket of paint and his brush and leveled a cool gaze on her.

She didn't stop working. Refused to even glance his way. But she could feel his eyes on her. That intense, steel-blue stare pierced through her body to its very core.

"Ridiculous," he muttered under his breath.

His voice had been a mere whisper, but she started at the sound of it. The rich reverberation of that one word started a chain reaction to occur inside her. Emotions heated and churned, like a pot of water just coming to a simmer. Suddenly she realized her hands trembled, her mouth grew dry, her heart raced like a runaway locomotive. Worse yet, the most feminine part of her, way down deep inside, seemed to sprout to life then and there. Like a dormant seed taking root and shooting up through the rich soil in the heat of spring.

She wanted him, damn it. She wanted him desperately.

Determined to hide this unexpected surge of desire, she swiveled her head and tossed him a quick look. "Did you say something?" she asked with as much nonchalance as she could muster.

She didn't want to respond to him verbally at all. The cumbersome silence had been awkward, but it was preferable to talking. However, she'd do anything to keep him from seeing her sudden physical and emotional response to him.

"I said—" his tone was louder as he clearly enunciated each word "—this is ridiculous."

The mask of confusion she donned was meant to express that she had no idea as to what he was referring.

"Oh, don't act like you haven't noticed it," he snapped. "The air between us is so thick it couldn't be cut with an ax."

Again, she gave him the briefest glance. "I don't know what you're talking about—"

"You're lying."

His accusation forced her to stop painting. She bent down, balancing the paint brush on the rim of the can. Raising up and squaring her shoulders, she asked, "What is it you want from me, Adam?"

She'd been about as prepared to hear the question that had tumbled from her lips as he seemed to be. A shadow crossed his handsome features, and his brow furrowed. It was then that she wondered—no, she *feared*—she'd revealed more about what was going on in her head than she had meant.

Rather than answer her query, he softly said, "I didn't mean to hurt your feelings yesterday, Hannah."

"Hurt my feelings?" The chuckle that erupted from her throat was raw around the edges. It didn't fool anyone, least of all Adam. She could tell that. Meaning to fix the damage, she said, "You didn't hurt me. I told you it was okay. And it is. I'm okay. *Everything is okay.*"

He looked at her. "No, it isn't," he told her. "You

know that isn't true." Then he sighed. His hands lowered from where he'd planted them on his hips, and he took a step toward her. "It's not that I don't want you. I do. Very much. You know I've been attracted to you since—"

"Stop!" She raised her hand, palm up, using it as a sort of shield. She didn't want him coming too close to her. If he were to touch her, she just might crumble into a million pieces right here on the lawn.

Crumble? a stubborn voice asked. *Am I going to let him make me fall to pieces?*

No! came a silent, stentorian reply.

However, a surge of elation battled with the bitterness and anger she felt. Hearing that Adam wanted her, that he was attracted to her, made her heart flutter with pure joy.

Are you crazy? the embittered, resentful part of her silently railed. This man wants you to give up your dream. For him! The heavy cloud of anger strangled and then completely snuffed out her moment of delight, leaving her feeling outright hostile.

"Do you think I don't know what you want?" She raked him with a scathing look. "You aren't willing to compromise. Or settle. I'm smart enough to have figured out that you want what every other man wants. *Everything.* And you won't be happy until you get it."

He grew still. "I can't speak for every man," he said, quietly. "I can only speak for me." He nodded. "And you're right. I don't want to settle. I tried that before and it didn't work. I was married to a woman who was self-centered, career oriented."

Just like you, his tone seemed to accuse.

"And although I tried to make it work," he continued, "it didn't. I had to walk away. So I won't settle again. Why should I? I *do* want it all. From a woman who isn't afraid to give it."

Anger rolled over her, threatening to drown her in its wake. "*Afraid?* You think I'm afraid?" She shook with fury. "I'm not afraid of anything. I won't give you everything because I *refuse* to give it."

A man will take and take and take. Her mother's complaint whispered through her head, firming Hannah's resolve, stoking her ire until it blazed red-hot.

"It's not fair for a man to take everything," Hannah said. "It's not fair for a man to leave a woman nothing for herself. My mother left this town because she refused to drown in Bobby Ray's neediness. In his laziness. In his lack of ambition. He refused to provide for her, so she had to provide for herself."

"You always talk about your mother as if she was and is so self-sacrificing." A lock of his raven hair fell across his brow as he shook his head in obvious incredulity. "Well, I say she was pretty damned selfish. So selfish that she ran off and left her husband and her baby daughter behind."

Hannah's jaw actually dropped open a full inch.

"There," he said, satisfaction squaring his shoulders, "I've said it. I've been thinking it since you first arrived. Now my feelings are out in the open."

"You don't have any idea what you're talking about," Hannah told him. "My mother left here to make a better life for herself—" Realizing what she said, she backed up to make a correction. "To make a better life for *both of us*."

"You don't believe that."

His quiet observation only served to stir her anger further. "I most certainly do."

"Then tell me why you came back to Little Haven."

"You know why."

"I want to hear you say it."

She shouldn't allow him to bait her, but she'd play his game. "To take care of Tammy."

"But Tammy's being taken care of. She always has been. She has plenty of people here who love her. Who watch out for her."

"Adam," she said, "my father died. Tammy needed someone here. To be with her. To help her through. To be her guardian."

"Bobby Ray had been dead for over a month before you showed up. Tammy was dealing with her grief just fine. So why did you come?"

His persistence with the same silly question grated on her.

"I've already answered that," she snapped at him.

"You haven't answered fully."

Plunking a fist on her hip, she said sarcastically, "Well, you obviously think you know more about why I came to Little Haven than I. Why don't you enlighten me?"

"I'll be happy to," he said. "You did come to take care of Tammy."

"Didn't I already say that?" she grumbled.

He ignored her caustic banter, "You came to take care of her because you needed to find out if she was being taken care of. If she *had been* taken care of all these years." His voice flattened. "Because you hadn't been."

"Hadn't been?" She shook her head in confusion, not immediately understanding what he was getting at.

"You wanted to know if Bobby Ray had loved and cared for Tammy," he explained. "You wanted to be assured that Tammy's life wasn't as hard...as yours."

"What?" The one-word query exposed her total amazement.

"You were never taken care of properly, Hannah." His tone had dropped to a hushed whisper, but she heard his every word, perfectly. "You were forced to take responsibility for yourself far too early. Your mother shoved you out of the nest before your wings had even formed."

"That's absurd!"

He shook his head. "No," he said. "No, it's not."

"My mother did what was in my best interest."

"Your mother did what was in *her* best interest," he insisted. "And it was in her best interest to lie to you about the circumstances surrounding why she left town all those years ago. It was in her best interest to cultivate in you priorities that are not, and never will be, conducive to your well-being." He used his fingers to comb back the lock of hair that had fallen over his forehead.

"My priorities are just fine, thank you very much," she said.

"Your priorities are about as mangled as they can be."

His criticism knocked the wind out of her. "Who do you think you are? I don't have to stand here and listen to this."

"Oh, yes, you do."

And there was some unreadable expression in his handsome face that forced her to stay put. She crossed her arms over her chest. Well, she might have to listen, but she didn't have to like it.

"All this talk of independence and self-reliance is fine," he went on, "but a person needs other people in her life. A person *needs* to rely on others just as much as others rely on her." He stuffed one fist into his pocket. "Your mother raised you to be independent, you say, because she wanted you to be able to stand on your own two feet. Well, I say she force-fed you on self-reliance, not for your own good, but so that you'd be out of her hair, out of her house, as soon as possible."

Hannah pressed her lips together, felt them grow bloodless. He was a raving lunatic, spouting off utter foolishness.

"If you'll allow yourself to think about what I've said," he continued, "I'm sure you'll come to agree with me."

"I won't."

She'd been sure her emphatic statement would have sparked anger in him, but it hadn't. His tone only seemed to grow more calm.

"Then let's go back to the reason you came to Little Haven," he said. "Let's talk about your obsession with taking care of Tammy—"

"O-obsession," she sputtered, highly offended.

He ignored her interruption, and his voice remained utterly tranquil as he said, "Better yet, let's talk about why you haven't been able to bring yourself to tell your sister that you plan to move her to New York."

The sudden urge to defend herself had Hannah stuttering, but she found she couldn't seem to form any coherent words.

"Even with all your talk of your big job promotion up north," he said, not waiting for her to respond. "Even with all your determination to be oh, so independent, you know down deep in your heart that taking Tammy away from Little Haven, away from the people who love her and care about her, is dead wrong."

Hannah's mind churned with turmoil. "I...I don't—" She stopped, swallowed. "I don't want to hear any more." Then she felt the need to protest. "It's not true. Any of it."

"But there's more, Hannah," he said.

She turned away and started for the house.

"There are more things you need to know," he called after her.

The steps of the back porch creaked under her feet.

"Things about your father. Misconceptions you have about him."

The rusty spring of the back screen door complained as she pulled on the knob.

"You don't have to take my word for it."

Hannah leaned against the kitchen counter, trembling from head to foot.

"Ask anyone in town."

She pressed her palms against her ears to block out his voice. She didn't want to hear any more. She didn't!

What Adam said shook the very foundation on which she'd built her life. Why was he trying to tear her down? She didn't understand why he wanted to hurt her so.

Before too long she heard the sound of his truck engine starting. She heard it fading as he drove away.

Hannah took a deep, calming breath. The truth was never anything to fear, was it? The truth only made a person stronger.

If there was any chance that she'd been raised on lies, then she needed to know about it. But could she handle discovering that her life was based on lies?

She was strong. She knew that about herself. But was she strong enough to handle the truth?

Expelling a shaky sigh, she realized she had to know what really went on all those years ago. And she knew just the person who could help her discover the truth.

Chapter Ten

"Honey—"

Mrs. Blake's palm was as soft and warm as kitten down, and just as comforting, as it slid overtop Hannah's cold hand.

"Let me get you a nice, tall glass of iced tea. You're obviously upset, and I surely didn't mean for that to happen."

"It's not your fault," Hannah said, her voice weak sounding, overwhelmed by all she'd learned. "I wanted to know. I *needed* to know."

The chrome legs of the old-fashioned kitchen chairs raked across the linoleum floor as Mrs. Blake got up and went to the cupboard for glasses. Her blindness seemed to cause her no hesitation.

The urge to go over the facts again rose up inside Hannah.

"So," she said. Pausing for only a moment, she continued, "My father wasn't on welfare?"

He wasn't lazy. He didn't lack ambition. Lord, how could she have judged her father so wrongly?

"No," Mrs. Blake said. She paused to cover her mouth with a tissue and cough, a residual symptom of her bout with bronchitis. "Those weren't welfare checks he received. That money came from Social Security due to his disability."

"And he got hurt falling off the roof of our house?" Hannah asked.

"Early on, your mother talked about nothing but her dreams of that house." Ice cubes tinkled as the elderly woman filled the glasses with tea from a pitcher. "And your father hammered in every nail just for her. The three of you moved in before it was even finished. Your mother was pregnant with Tammy at the time."

Mrs. Blake brought the glasses to the table and set one directly in front of Hannah.

"After your father's accident," Mrs. Blake continued, "things were bad. Everybody in town had hoped that once the baby was born, the situation would brighten. But it didn't. Tammy came into the world and wasn't here but a couple of months before the doctors were giving your mother more bad news."

Her brown, wrinkled fingers curled around the glass, but Mrs. Blake didn't pick it up. Instead, she went on talking. "Your mother actually came to see me one day. Said she didn't think she had the strength to stay here. That taking care of a husband who couldn't work and a baby who would never grow up was just too much for her. I knew then that she'd leave. But I have to admit that she surprised me when she took you with her."

"Oh?"

The woman's head bobbed. "I was sure she'd cut herself free of all three of you and fly off like a bird."

How I wish she had. The thought flitted through Hannah's mind, making her eyes go wide with surprise.

"It was so obvious that she was running from responsibility, so when she took you with her it was confusing to everyone." Mrs. Blake did pause long enough to take a sip of tea. After she swallowed, she smiled. "Guilt. That's what I decided it was. She wouldn't have been able to live with the guilt of leaving all of you behind. So she took one with her. The one who would need the least from her."

"So Bobby Ray didn't choose Tammy over me." Hannah's unexpected words came out in a husky whisper.

"Choose?" The old woman chuckled. "He had no choice in this matter at all." Then she shook her head. "Is that what you've thought all this time? That your daddy chose for you to go? For Tammy to stay?"

"Well…"

It wasn't an idea Hannah had ever allowed herself to actually verbalize, but the thought had danced around in the back of her mind.

"Bobby Ray loved you." Mrs. Blake's tone brooked no argument.

"Even though I felt a little jealous, I was always kind of glad that Tammy was the one who got to stay," Hannah said, surprised that she was exposing so much of her thoughts and feelings to this woman. "Daddy was…softer. From what I remember, anyway. He was more loving than Mother. And even if he'd have had to institutionalize Tammy, I knew he'd visit her often and let her know she was loved." Her voice took on a faraway quality as she said, "Yes, he was much more loving, more giving, than Mother."

Mrs. Blake's soft laughter erupted. "That observation doesn't surprise me." Then she said, "Like I said, he loved you, child. He kept up with what was happening in your life as best he could."

Hannah nodded. She'd been shocked to hear how her father had faithfully subscribed to the small Staten Island newspaper featuring personal and professional accomplishments of local residents. She could only remember a few times that her name had made the paper, but knowing that her father had searched for information about her really warmed her heart, made her feel cherished. Just like a father is supposed to make his daughter feel.

"I'll look for the clippings when I get home," Hannah promised. Noticing the time, she got up from the table. "I really should be going."

"But you haven't even touched your tea."

Mrs. Blake might not be able to see, but she sure didn't miss a trick.

"I'm sorry," Hannah said. "But it's nearly dinnertime, and Tammy will be wondering what happened to me."

"Well, you go on, then," the woman said. "But before you go, I want to thank you again for taking care of me when I was sick."

"Mrs. Blake, you've already thanked me," Hannah told her. "Besides, no thanks are necessary. Like I told you before, I was more than happy to be here with you."

And as Hannah said the words, she realized she'd never spoken anything with more sincerity.

As soon as Hannah arrived home, she began searching for the newspaper clippings her father had saved. The drawers of the end tables in the living room had contained a couple of dull-pointed pencils, a pen or two, an outdated map of Delaware and a few other odds and ends. She went through the small desk and found nothing more than old bill receipts and some paperclips.

It wasn't really necessary for her to actually find the clippings. Hannah believed Mrs. Blake. But actually seeing them, actually having the newspaper articles in her hands would make the facts all the more real. It meant so much to her to imagine her father sitting down and reading the paper, scanning the small *Staten Island News* for snippets of information regarding his oldest daughter.

Moving to the bookcase, she shook her head at the sight of all the clutter. She'd kept up with the dusting, but that's all she'd done since she'd been so busy trying to get the outside of the house painted and the yard in some sort of order. She smiled when she thought of Tammy's aversion to housework. Would she ever get the house ready to sell? she wondered.

But now that you know Bobby Ray built this house with his own hands, with the sweat of his brow, the thought flashed through her head like an unexpected bolt of lightning, do you really *want* to sell?

The sentimental query went unanswered as she lifted the cover of an old photo album. Her inhalation was short and sharp. She'd found the clippings. Her father *had* kept up with her. Just as Mrs. Blake had said. He'd lovingly cut out the tiny articles, two of which actually contained pictures of her, and tucked them away for safekeeping.

Tears blurred her vision so that she couldn't even read the words on the yellowed newsprint. Why hadn't he written her? Why hadn't he called? She would never know the answer to those questions.

She frowned. Maybe he *had* tried to contact her, and her mother had thwarted his efforts. Knowing her mother, Hannah believed she'd probably never discover the real truth. Guilt literally poured onto her shoulders like a thick layer of concrete.

Why hadn't *she* written him? Why hadn't *she* picked up her phone and tried to reach him?

Because she'd been too wrapped up in herself, that's why.

Pressing the clipped articles to her chest, Hannah exhaled a shaky sigh. She missed her chance to know her father. She would regret that for the rest of her life.

Hannah's ears perked, her head turning sharply at the sound of Tammy's sobs. She heard her sister's arrival before the back screen door even had a chance to open.

Slipping the newspaper articles back into the album, Hannah shot to her feet and ran for the kitchen.

"What is it, honey?" She reached out and grasped Tammy's shoulders. "What happened? Are you hurt?"

"My money." Tammy's whole body quivered. "My money's all gone."

Confusion bit deeply into Hannah's brow. "What money, sweetheart? What are you talking about?"

Instead of answering, Tammy groaned, covered her face with her hands as though she wanted to hide.

Hannah guided her to the kitchen table and then nudged her to sit. "I want you to calm down, honey. I can't help you if I don't know what's going on."

"You'll be mad at me."

Shaking her head, Hannah gently assured her, "No, I won't. I promise. Now, I need you to talk to me." When Tammy refused to look at her, she begged, "Please, honey. Let me help you."

Finally her sister raised her innocent green eyes, and the sadness in them ripped at Hannah's heart.

"My money came today." Tammy's voice was as jagged as broken glass. "When my money comes, I always go right to the bank. Just like Daddy and Adam told me to."

"Ah," Hannah breathed. Now she knew what Tammy was speaking of. Her monthly check had arrived from the state.

Huge tears welled up in her sister's eyes and then spilled over to trail down her already-damp cheeks. "But now it's gone. It's all gone."

"You lost it?" Hannah asked.

Tammy shook her head, fear wrinkling the usually smooth-as-satin skin on her forehead. She averted her gaze.

Capturing her sister's chin between her fingers, Hannah gently forced Tammy to look at her. "Tell me," she quietly coaxed.

"He took it," Tammy said. "The man took all my money."

Hannah's heart pounded. "Who, honey? You were robbed? Did he hurt you? Are you okay?" The questions popped from her mouth like the short jabs of a professional boxer. She inspected Tammy as she asked them.

There were no bruises or scratches visible on her sister's delicate skin, no tears in her clothing. But still Hannah felt frantic. When Tammy hesitated too long, Hannah's frustration got the best of her.

"Please, Tammy," she said, her tone firmer and louder than even she expected, "tell me who took your money."

Fresh teardrops fell down her sister's face. "I knew you'd be mad."

"I'm not angry. I'm worried."

Tammy swallowed, gazed at her a moment and then said, "He didn't really take it. I...I gave it to him."

"You gave him your money." She repeated Tammy's words to give herself time to assimilate the information. "Who was the man, Tammy?"

Her shrug was nearly imperceptible. In a tiny voice, she said, "I don't know who he is. I hadn't ever seen him before."

Someone from out of town, Hannah mused.

"He said he needed money," Tammy continued. "He said he was hungry. That his kids were hungry. He asked me where he could go for help. I told him I had some money. I wanted to help him." Another worried frown creased the tiny space between Tammy's brows. "I watched him drive off. And I felt so good. So happy. I helped that man." She sighed. "But then...all of the sudden...I remembered that I needed my money. That I would need to buy food. And pay for my telephone." Her chin quivered. "I wish I had kept some of my money. But now it's all gone. I'm just like that man. I need money. I need help."

Despair and utter sorrow pulsed from Tammy, and Hannah didn't think she could stand the empathy that wrenched her insides so painfully. Her whole chest filled up with the raw emotion, it closed off her throat until she thought she'd surely suffocate.

How had this awful thing happened? When had it happened? While she was arguing with Adam? When she was selfishly discussing the past with Mrs. Blake? Whenever Tammy's ordeal had taken place, whenever the man had talked her out of her check, Hannah hadn't been where she *should* have been. She wasn't watching over her sister.

This was her own fault, Hannah knew. She'd wanted so desperately to take care of Tammy. She'd put her job, her whole life, on hold in order to see that Tammy was okay. But now she was discovering that she'd failed. Miserably.

Already blue and terribly depressed about finding out she'd been so wrong about her father, Hannah felt the weight of even more gloom descend on her. It was too much. The task of caring for Tammy was too big for her. She just couldn't handle it. She needed help. Desperately.

At that moment Hannah realized that her idea of taking Tammy north with her, placing her sister in a home where she'd be safe and secure from those who would harm her, really was the one-and-only solution to this problem. In a special facility, Tammy would be protected by an entire staff of state-paid workers who were trained to do the very job that Hannah knew now she was incapable of doing.

Hannah wasn't the kind of person to easily admit defeat, but she had no choice. Not when Tammy's safety was at stake. She could have been hurt by that man who had accosted her today. She could have been maimed. Or worse yet, murdered. Evil people did those kinds of things every day for the few dollars or sometimes just the pocket change carried by their victims.

Her body physically quaked with fear and trepidation. She wouldn't let Tammy be hurt. She wouldn't.

She needed to talk to a lawyer. Now.

She glanced at the clock on the wall. It was nearly six. Surely that lawyer—what was his name? She frantically searched her memory. The one who had sent the letter informing her mother of Bobby Ray's death. Henry Tillis, she remembered. Surely he'd left his office for the day. But maybe not. Maybe he was still working.

"Everything's going to be all right," Hannah assured Tammy. And then she went to get her purse to search for the man's phone number.

"You sit out here," Hannah told her sister, and then watched as Tammy settled into one of the upholstered chairs in the small waiting area. "I'm going in to speak to Mr. Tillis. I won't be long."

Hannah knew it had been a miracle when she'd called Henry Tillis and found him still in his office. Her urgent request that he see her—*now*—had been met with no opposition, even though she hadn't had the opportunity yet of making the man's acquaintance.

Since the lawyer's receptionist had evidently gone home for the day, Hannah knocked on the door to the inner office to announce herself. She entered only after he called out for her to do so.

"Miss Cavanaugh," he said, standing and offering her his outstretched hand in greeting.

She crossed the room, took his hand and shook it. "Hello, Mr. Tillis. It was awfully nice of you to see me on such short notice."

"Not at all," he said. "But I must insist that you call me Hank."

Hannah guessed he was in his mid-forties. He had a nice smile. His slightly sagging jowls and deep-set brown eyes reminded her of a hound dog, loyal and intelligent.

She grinned. "I'll call you Hank if you'll call me Hannah."

He indicated that she take a seat. "What can I do for you, Hannah?"

"Well—"

The one small word was all she'd expelled before the door behind her opened.

"Tammy, honey," she said over her shoulder, "I asked you to wait—"

"It's not Tammy."

The rich timbre of Adam's voice had her gasping, jerking to her feet and turning to face him.

"Hank," Adam greeted the lawyer, then his cool blue eyes locked once again on her.

What was he doing here? she wondered, but the question remained locked deep in her thoughts.

"What are you doing here, Hannah?"

Hearing him voice the very question that rang through her own head like the peal of a bell made Hannah feel eerie...like some strange psychic connection linked their thoughts.

Don't be silly, she chided herself.

"Not that it's any of your business," she told Adam stiffly, knowing full well he wouldn't react favorably to her answer, "but I've come to see Mr. Tillis about having myself named as Tammy's guardian. I want to have her state check sent to me. Something needs to be done. As soon as possible—"

"You can't do that," Adam said. "Not without having Tammy declared incompetent."

The look she gave him revealed that what he'd just stated was exactly her intention.

He glanced over his shoulder, evidently at Tammy, although Hannah couldn't see her sister from where she stood. Then Adam stepped into the office, closing the door softly behind him. When he looked at Hannah, the coolness in his steel-blue eyes had turned to chips of solid ice.

"I won't let you do this. I made a promise to Bobby Ray to look after Tammy. I won't break my word."

The quiet tone of his voice didn't disguise the intensity of his conviction.

Anger flared up in Hannah, a white-hot flame that sizzled and crackled with blazing heat. Why couldn't he see that she was only doing this for Tammy?

"She's my sister," Hannah said through gritted teeth. "She's *my* responsibility."

She recognized his anger, saw that his matched her own. Hannah didn't really believe she owed him any explanations whatsoever. But she did know, had learned over these past weeks, that he cared about Tammy. And for that reason alone she decided she'd go a little further in clarifying her actions.

"Adam," she said, trying but failing to keep the plea for understanding from her voice, "she lost her check. A month's worth of income gone—" she snapped her fingers "—just like that."

His handsome chin tipped up. "So? Lots of people can't handle money. That doesn't mean she's incompetent. Bad things happen. In everybody's life. Tammy's no different."

Pursing her lips, she shook her head, the tiny motion conveying her disagreement with him. His jaw clenched, his whole body tensing with what Hannah perceived as stubbornness.

"I won't let you do this," he repeated.

Irritation got the best of her. "And what are you going to do to stop me?" she snapped. "Who's going to listen to a down-and-out handyman? What could you possibly argue against—"

"Is that how you've seen me all this time?"

A deep frown formed between his eyes, and Hannah instantly felt bad that she'd offended him. But she didn't retract her opinion. She couldn't. Tammy's welfare was at stake here.

"Do you seriously believe," he finally said, "that the court would allow a felon to act as Tammy's guardian?"

"What..." Hannah mouthed the word, not even sure she'd voiced it.

Adam looked at Hank. "She broke the law. Practiced nursing here in Delaware without a license."

Her inhalation was filled with disbelief. "How dare you use that against me! I took care of Mrs. Blake *for you*. You begged me to do that."

At that instant—the worst possible moment, as far as Hannah was concerned—she was hit with a realization. She had *enjoyed* nursing Mrs. Blake. She had received more satisfaction from doing it than she had in all the years she'd worked in New York. And there were a few reasons for that. Tammy loved Mrs. Blake, had talked about her with great affection. And the elderly, blind lady had loved Tammy. But most of all Hannah now understood that the deep gratification she'd experienced had come from the fact that she'd been able to help alleviate Adam's concern for the ill woman.

Well, after this fiasco of a situation, she'd never in a million years allow Adam to learn how she felt.

He raised his dark brows and said, "Don't you think *begged* is a little strong? You make it sound as if I got down on my hands and knees and—"

"Okay," Hank said from where he now stood behind his desk, "let's calm down here a minute."

Turmoil churned in Hannah's head. She didn't know whether to explain to the lawyer her side of these horrible charges or if she should whack Adam full on the chest with her purse. The man was insufferable!

Hank's hound dog cheeks jerked once before he garnered control of his smile. He cleared his throat, tugged on the lapels of his sport coat, evidently giving himself time to contain his humor. Hannah felt miserably embarrassed that she'd allowed herself to get so caught up in her argument with Adam in this man's office.

"Now, we're not in a courtroom here," Hank reminded them. "And I'm not a judge. We're not going to solve any of our problems by shouting at each other or pointing fingers of recrimination."

Hannah fought the urge to lower her gaze. How could she have acted so childishly? Because Adam had pushed her into it, that's why. She shot him a quick glare.

The lawyer focused his attention on Hannah, and she gave him the courtesy of her unwavering concentration.

"Incompetence isn't something that's easy to prove," he said. "But if you're determined to do this, I'll get the proper paperwork in order. However, I have to warn you, character witnesses are a big part of such a hearing. And as Little Haven's mayor, Adam will make a formidable witness. His testimony..."

The rest of the lawyer's lecture fell on deaf ears. Hannah turned to Adam. "You're—" Her head tilted a fraction. "But why didn't you tell me?"

He seemed to enjoy her state of confusion. With a shrug he said, "It never came up."

All those mornings he refused to come to paint! Now she understood.

"You spend your mornings—"

"Fulfilling my mayoral duties," he supplied.

"Most afternoons I'm able to volunteer my time to helping friends."

She tisked, disgustedly. "You didn't volunteer your time to paint my house," she accused.

Again he shrugged. "You offered to pay me. But you can rest assured that I donated every penny to the Methodist soup kitchen."

"Look you two..." Hank rounded his desk. "Neither of you are going to get anywhere in court fighting each other. Why don't you take some time to talk about Tammy's situation? If you don't mind, Hannah, I'm going to take your sister across the street for a hamburger. You and Adam can come over there and join us in a while."

He closed his office door behind him, leaving Hannah and Adam all alone.

Silent seconds ticked by, stretching and straining the atmosphere around them until it was so taut, so tight she was sure that the molecules in the air would begin to clash and shatter, that they would spark into vibrant red fireworks. Finally she could take the tension no more!

"You were right, okay?" she said, unable to control the force with which she projected the question at him. "You were right about everything you said this afternoon. Is that what you want to hear me say? Well, I'm saying it. Are you happy now?"

"Being right wasn't my motive," he quietly informed her.

But she was too stirred up to believe him.

"My mother left Little Haven because she didn't want to be dragged down by Bobby Ray." She swiped wildly at the bangs that brushed her forehead.

"Or by Tammy. And Mrs. Blake is sure that the only reason my mother took me along with her is because she'd have never been able to live with the guilt of leaving all of us behind. So she took me." Hannah poked herself in the chest. "Me. The healthy one. The one who would need the least attention. The one who could shoulder her own load. Whether I was ready to shoulder the load or not."

Her breath was coming in great heaves, her distress was so huge, as she finally acknowledged the anger and bitterness she felt toward her mother.

"And you were right to tell me I had things to learn about my father," she said. "Bobby Ray wasn't a lazy good-for-nothing. He was loving. He was gentle. He was kind. And I didn't have to be told that. I remembered that. From the whispery memories floating around in my head. Memories I'd pushed aside because it hurt too much to bring them into the light of day." She stopped only long enough to moisten her cottony lips. "I was glad Tammy was the one who got to stay behind," she admitted. "She needed to be loved. Needed his gentleness. His kindness. My sister wouldn't have survived living around my mother. That would have been absolute hell for her." Hannah's laughter possessed a glass-shard edge that had nothing whatsoever to do with humor. "That's even if my mother would have had her around, which she wouldn't have."

She paced the length of the office, first away from Adam, then a few steps toward him. "It was awful." She felt as if in her own little world as she reminisced about the past. "My life was so damned hard. Working all the time. Giving *her* most of my money. Trying to go to school. Struggling to survive. Never receiving guidance in anything. And then having my choices criticized at every turn."

"Hannah."

But she didn't even hear his comforting tone. Her shoulders sagged, and she looked up at him. "You were also right about why I came to Little Haven. I wanted to take care of Tammy *because nobody ever took care of me.*"

A lump formed in her throat, but she tried hard to swallow it. She had more to say, and she needed to say it before she broke down and cried.

"But I learned something else today, Adam," she said. "As capable as I am, as independent and self-reliant as I've been forced to be, I'm still not competent enough to give Tammy all that she needs."

"Oh, love—" his voice was still and soft "—of course you can."

"Now there's where you're wrong. Very wrong." There was no anger in her now. Only sadness. A deep, abiding sadness. She sighed. "I can't be with her twenty-four hours a day. That's what she needs." Her jaw lifted, resolutely. "That's what she'll get in a special facility."

He shook his head, but Hannah was tired of fighting with him so she said nothing.

"But will she be happy?" he asked. Without waiting for an answer, he continued, "Hannah, she's survived nearly twenty-five years without round-the-clock guards. She's a free spirit. A beautiful spirit. And that spirit will be crushed if you put her…"

The rest of his thought faded, and Hannah got the distinct impression that the idea of putting Tammy in a home for people with special needs was so abhorrent to him that he couldn't even bring himself to voice the thought.

"I asked you early on," he said, his words curiously controlled, "why you wouldn't want Tammy's life to be full. Rich. Rich with love and relationships and experiences. She's not my family. I know that. But I want the absolute best for her. I want her to try everything. To experience the pleasure. Endure the pain. To partake of all the intricate textures life has to offer." He looked at her, frustration clear in his gaze. "What else is living for?"

He meant well. She knew that. And she couldn't fault him for his views. But his good intentions didn't make him any less wrong.

"You don't understand," she told him. "She was approached today by a man who took all her money." She shook her head, correcting herself, "Tammy *gave* him every penny she had. It was a miracle she wasn't hurt, Adam. She could have been raped, or murdered." A fearful shiver coursed across her skin. "It was just a miracle she wasn't." She murmured the aside.

She sighed, hating what she was about to admit. Hating the truth that she had to make him understand. "I'm not able to take care of Tammy. And neither are you. We can't be there in every instance. We just can't. And the situation with that man today proves my point beyond a shadow of a doubt."

Reaching into his pocket, he extracted a small slip of paper. He came closer, his whole expression brightening with an obvious spark of excitement.

"We're going to find him."

"Find him?" she asked. "You know who this man is? But Tammy told me he was a stranger."

Adam darted a quick glance at the paper he held, then he looked at her. "James Welford, he delivers the mail in town, saw Tammy talking to a man this afternoon. Someone he'd never seen before. He wasn't too concerned, but just as a precaution he jotted down the man's license number."

"We have a plate number?"

One corner of his sexy mouth curled upward slightly. "James happened to mention it to Tom from the hardware store. When Tammy passed his store window crying, Tom called me right away. I was on my way back to your house when I saw your car parked in front of Hank's office."

Everyone's concern for Tammy made Hannah's lips broaden with gratitude. But her smile quickly faded. "I don't want you to think I'm unappreciative, but the fact that we might, and I stress the word *might*, get Tammy's check back changes nothing. Taking care of her...keeping her safe is too big a job for me. I can't possibly do it alone."

"You're not alone." Hurt clouded his gorgeous gray-blue eyes. "Everyone in this town is behind you, helping you." He lifted the slip of paper he held in his fingers. "If this doesn't prove it to you, I don't know what will."

Her exhalation was desolate. "Facing life on my own is all I've ever known." She took a moment to absently nibble her bottom lip as she gazed off into one corner of the room. "Every challenge, every problem, every success, I've worked through alone."

"Success," he murmured, disgust evident in the

word. "I understand now. That damned job promotion up north is more important to you than—"

"No!" She shot him a furious look. "My life in New York has nothing whatsoever to do with why I came to see Hank. Tammy's welfare is all I'm concerned with."

The indignation left her just as quickly as it had flared, and she shook her head sadly. "But I have to tell you, Adam. I can't see myself staying here. I'm on a path. A path of my own choosing. A path I've worked hard for."

"But you chose the path you're on before you got to know Tammy," he told her.

She only hesitated a second before giving him a tiny nod in agreement. He was right about that.

"So," he went on quietly, "step off the path you're on. Change direction. Start down another path. One that will lead you to Tammy." Sudden, intense emotion turned his eyes the perfect color of fine delft. "One that will lead you to me."

A shudder quivered deliciously through her whole body, heating her blood, making her go weak all over. But a lifetime of wariness, years of total independence, refused to allow her to move or to speak.

"I want you, Hannah." Then he oh, so softly added, "I love you."

He was the biggest temptation she'd ever faced in her life. She wanted him, too. And, my, how she loved him. But...

"I'm afraid." The whispered statement was the utter truth. "I...I don't want to lose myself in a...in a..."

"Relationship," he supplied.

They stared at each other, then his jaw tensed in obvious frustration.

"Hannah, I've tried in as many ways as I know how to show you what's important in life. I urged you from the very start to get to know your sister. I asked you to take care of Mrs. Blake when she was sick. I wanted you to get to know Tammy's beau. I tried to get close to you myself." He shifted his weight from one foot to the other. "I did that because I wanted you to understand what I've come to see. That relationships are the most important things in life."

The light from the overhead fixture glinted off his ebony hair as he shook his head. "I mean, a person can have professional success, fame and fortune, but without people, without loving relationships, life would be empty."

Finally finding her tongue, Hannah said, "I know that now. I do understand that." She took a deep breath. "I'm not afraid of loving Tammy. Or Mrs. Blake. Or Brian." Then she stammered, "B-but I *am* afraid of loving you."

Nothing would change the fact that she loved him—desperately. However, she did feel the need to voice her apprehension.

Adam's tone became as gentle as a caress. "You seem to think that being involved with me would somehow snuff out your identity."

She knew her ingrained fear was reflected in her gaze.

"Honey," he continued, "a loving relationship shouldn't change you. It should *enhance* you. Make you better." He grinned. "Falling in love with you has sure made me a better person."

Still she hesitated.

Then he said, "You're worried about becoming dependent, aren't you? I can't promise you that it won't happen. In fact, I hope that it does. I *want* you to depend on me...just as much as I plan to depend on you."

His idea of what love was supposed to be seemed so foreign to her. So different from what she'd been led to understand. So alien. So beautiful.

She wanted to believe him. Wanted to trust him. And she could literally feel all her fears and inhibitions changing, metamorphosing like a drab caterpillar magically turning into a colorful butterfly.

Surrender must have shown in her expression, because Adam smiled, a wide and loving smile that would have transformed her idea of intimate relationships no matter how dismal it had been. They came together then, both stepping forward to fall into each other's arms.

"I love you, Adam," she whispered frantically in his ear.

"I love you, too."

Leaning away from him, she shot him a look filled with teasing censure. "Why, then, did you try to get me into trouble? Why did you tell Hank that I'd nursed Mrs. Blake?"

"Well..." His tone was candid, sincere. "You did."

She gasped, glaring at him, and he laughed, a rich, vibrant, velvety sound that had her unwittingly splaying her hand across his chest so she could *feel* the sound of it.

"Besides," he said, lightly, "you're so beautiful when your eyes spark with irritation."

Then he tugged her against him, and she surrendered, burying her face in his neck and hugging him tightly. She felt light, buoyant, joyous. And she knew at that moment that shedding her independence, slipping out of the heavy burden of complete and total self-reliance would be the best thing that ever happened to her.

With Adam by her side, with his love to bolster and sustain her, Hannah felt certain she could conquer any obstacle, overcome any problem, whether it be crushing her well-learned, intrinsic fears about love or taking care of her sister.

"We *can* handle anything, can't we?" she whispered, pressing her hands on either side of his handsome face. "Together."

He nodded, love shining bright in his gray-blue eyes. "Together we can."

Then he pressed his lips to hers, his luscious kiss promising a ton of faith, a world of hope...and an entire lifetime of love.

Epilogue

There was something wonderful, something *magical,* about the smell of a newborn baby. Hannah smiled lovingly at the child she cradled carefully in her hands. The warm water in the plastic tub lapped at the infant's soft, pearly skin, making him gurgle with glee.

So much had happened in the two years since she'd made that fateful trip from New York to Little Haven. The Cavanaugh sisters' double wedding had been the event of the year with businesses all over town actually closing so the owners and their employees could attend and witness their mayor's exchanging of vows. The new medical clinic had celebrated its first anniversary, and Hannah had never felt so professionally fulfilled than when she was keeping track of the health records of the elderly residents of Little Haven or scheduling routine immunizations for the children of economically less fortunate families, people about whom she had come to care deeply.

Her life had changed so thoroughly, so completely, that she doubted her mother would even recognize her anymore. Hannah only smiled sadly now as she thought of her mother, a woman whose selfishness was blinding her to the true gifts life had to offer: the heartfelt and intimate love shared between a man and woman and the warm, tender bonds of devoted family and friends.

A fat drop of water rolled down the baby's temple, his little arms jerking outward in surprise.

"It's okay," Hannah crooned softly, gently rinsing away the last evidence of soap. "You're safe. And you're all clean."

She lifted him from the bath water and immediately handed him to Tammy, who waited nearby with a fluffy towel.

"And that," Hannah told her sister, "is how you bathe your new son."

Brian, Tammy's husband, smoothed gentle fingers over the baby's delicate toes.

"He looks just like you," Hannah said to her brother-in-law. She smiled when the young man's face beamed with pride. "Now you two take him into the living room and get him dried off, diapered and dressed for bed."

"This little baby boy," Tammy whispered, her voice filled with wonder, "is my one weakness."

"Mine, too," Brian added.

They went off, clinging together and to their new son, parental love and protection evident in every careful step. Moppet mewed, the orange tabby following close on their heels.

Only then did Hannah look across the table at her own adoring husband. He smiled at her in that way that never ceased to make her heart race with love and longing.

"Our little nephew is a real miracle," he murmured.

The unmistakable awe she heard in his hushed tone made one corner of her mouth twitch with loving endearment. Without thought, she reached out for him with one hand, sliding the other over her protruding belly.

"Well, I do hope you were paying attention to the lesson," she said, unable to keep the excited anticipation from shining in her eyes, "because you'll be bathing and diapering your own little miracle soon."

* * * * *

Of all the unforgettable families created by #1 *New York Times* bestselling author

NORA ROBERTS

the Donovans are the most extraordinary. For, along with their irresistible appeal, they've inherited some rather remarkable gifts from their Celtic ancestors.

Coming in November 1999

Enchanted

Available at your favorite retail outlet.

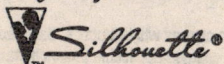

Silhouette®

Visit us at www.romance.net

SIMENCH

If you enjoyed what you just read,
then we've got an offer you can't resist!

Take 2 bestselling love stories FREE!
Plus get a FREE surprise gift!

Clip this page and mail it to Silhouette Reader Service™

IN U.S.A.	IN CANADA
3010 Walden Ave.	P.O. Box 609
P.O. Box 1867	Fort Erie, Ontario
Buffalo, N.Y. 14240-1867	L2A 5X3

YES! Please send me 2 free Silhouette Romance® novels and my free surprise gift. Then send me 6 brand-new novels every month, which I will receive months before they're available in stores. In the U.S.A., bill me at the bargain price of $2.90 plus 25¢ delivery per book and applicable sales tax, if any*. In Canada, bill me at the bargain price of $3.25 plus 25¢ delivery per book and applicable taxes**. That's the complete price and a savings of over 10% off the cover prices—what a great deal! I understand that accepting the 2 free books and gift places me under no obligation ever to buy any books. I can always return a shipment and cancel at any time. Even if I never buy another book from Silhouette, the 2 free books and gift are mine to keep forever. So why not take us up on our invitation. You'll be glad you did!

215 SEN CNE7
315 SEN CNE9

Name _____ (PLEASE PRINT)

Address _____ Apt.#

City _____ State/Prov. _____ Zip/Postal Code

* Terms and prices subject to change without notice. Sales tax applicable in N.Y.
** Canadian residents will be charged applicable provincial taxes and GST.
All orders subject to approval. Offer limited to one per household.
® are registered trademarks of Harlequin Enterprises Limited.

SROM99 ©1998 Harlequin Enterprises Limited

THE FORTUNES OF TEXAS

Membership in this family has its privileges...and its price. But what a fortune can't buy, a true-bred Texas love is sure to bring!

Coming in November 1999...

Expecting... In Texas
by
MARIE FERRARELLA

Wrangler Cruz Perez's night of passion with Savannah Clark had left the beauty pregnant with his child. Cruz's cowboy code of honor demanded he do right by the expectant mother, but could he convince Savannah—and himself—that his offer of marriage was inspired by true love?

THE FORTUNES OF TEXAS continues with **A Willing Wife** by Jackie Merritt, available in December 1999 from Silhouette Books.

Available at your favorite retail outlet.

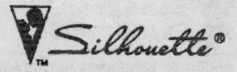

Silhouette®

Visit us at www.romance.net

PSFOT3

Silhouette Romance® and Silhouette Special Edition® welcome you to a heartwarming miniseries full of family traditions, scandalous secrets and newfound love.

With These Rings

by
PATRICIA THAYER

THE SECRET MILLIONAIRE (June '99)
Silhouette Special Edition®
A sweet-talkin' Texas oilman is just itching to transform this sexy single mom into Cinderella!

HER SURPRISE FAMILY (September '99)
Silhouette Romance®
To this bachelor, marriage is The Great Surrender. Will he wage war with his feelings...or give up his heart to the new lady in town?

THE MAN, THE RING, THE WEDDING (December '99)
Silhouette Romance®
Would a shocking family secret prevent two star-crossed lovers from making their own family...together?

Available at your favorite retail outlet.

Silhouette®

Look us up on-line at: http://www.romance.net   SSERINGS

Don't miss Silhouette's newest cross-line promotion,

Four royal sisters find their own Prince Charmings as they embark on separate journeys to find their missing brother, the Crown Prince!

Royally Wed

The search begins in October 1999 and continues through February 2000:

On sale October 1999: **A ROYAL BABY ON THE WAY**
by award-winning author **Susan Mallery** (Special Edition)

On sale November 1999: **UNDERCOVER PRINCESS**
by bestselling author **Suzanne Brockmann** (Intimate Moments)

On sale December 1999: **THE PRINCESS'S WHITE KNIGHT**
by popular author **Carla Cassidy** (Romance)

On sale January 2000: **THE PREGNANT PRINCESS**
by rising star **Anne Marie Winston** (Desire)

On sale February 2000: **MAN...MERCENARY...MONARCH**
by top-notch talent **Joan Elliott Pickart** (Special Edition)

ROYALLY WED
Only in—
SILHOUETTE BOOKS

Available at your favorite retail outlet.

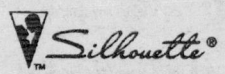

Silhouette®

Visit us at www.romance.net

SSERW

No one can anticipate the unexpected,
be it lust, love or larceny...

SOMETHING TO HIDE

Two exciting full-length novels by

TESS GERRITSEN

and

LYNN ERICKSON

Intrigue and romance are combined in this thrilling collection of heart-stopping adventure with a guaranteed happy ending.

Available October 1999 at your favorite retail outlet.

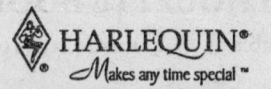

HARLEQUIN®
Makes any time special ™

Visit us at www.romance.net

PSBR21099

Silhouette ROMANCE™

VIRGIN BRIDES

Your favorite authors tell more heartwarming stories of lovely brides who discover love... for the first time....

July 1999 GLASS SLIPPER BRIDE
Arlene James (SR #1379)

Bodyguard Jack Keller had to protect innocent Jillian Waltham—day and night. But when his assignment became a matter of temporary marriage, would Jack's hardened heart need protection...from Jillian, his glass slipper bride?

September 1999 MARRIED TO THE SHEIK
Carol Grace (SR #1391)

Assistant Emily Claybourne secretly loved her boss, and now Sheik Ben Ali had finally asked her to marry him! But Ben was only interested in a temporary union...until Emily started showing him the joys of marriage—and love....

November 1999 THE PRINCESS AND THE COWBOY
Martha Shields (SR #1403)

When runaway Princess Josephene Francoeur needed a short-term husband, cowboy Buck Buchanan was the perfect choice. But to wed him, Josephene had to tell a *few* white lies, which worked...until "Josie Freeheart" realized she wanted to love her rugged cowboy groom forever!

Available at your favorite retail outlet.

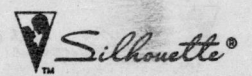

Silhouette®

Look us up on-line at: http://www.romance.net

SRVB992

Silhouette ROMANCE™

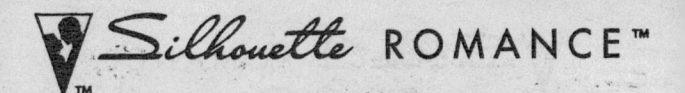

Join *Silhouette Romance* as more couples experience the joy only babies can bring!

Bundles of Joy

September 1999
THE BABY BOND
by Lilian Darcy (SR #1390)

Tom Callahan a daddy? Impossible! Yet that was before Julie Gregory showed up with the shocking news that she carried his child. Now the father-to-be knew marriage was the answer!

October 1999
BABY, YOU'RE MINE
by Lindsay Longford (SR #1396)

Marriage was the *last* thing on Murphy Jones's mind when he invited beautiful—and pregnant—Phoebe McAllister to stay with him. But then she and her newborn bundle filled his house with laughter...and had bachelor Murphy rethinking his no-strings lifestyle....

And in December 1999, popular author

MARIE FERRARELLA

brings you

THE BABY BENEATH THE MISTLETOE (SR #1408)

Available at your favorite retail outlet.

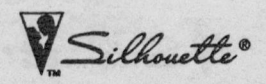

Silhouette®

Look us up on-line at: http://www.romance.net

SRBOJS-D